MW01139716

Sue -

Happily ever

after does exist!

XOXO

KA

Berg

Freed

An Uninhibited Series Novella

BOOK THREE OF THE UNINHIBITED SERIES

K.A. BERG

Freed

K.A. Berg

The following book contains mature themes, strong language, and sexual content. It is intended for mature audiences only.

Editor: Leslie Lewis
Cover Design: TE Black Designs
ISBN: 978-1976591464

Dedication

To all my wonderful readers who have loved Tanner and Ashley as much as me….

This one's for you!

Remember happily ever after's can happen in real life too! You just have to work for it. Nothing worth having comes easy.

Chapter One

ASHLEY

TANNER DROPS TO his knees and presses his soft, full, luscious lips to my belly. He lingers there a moment before pulling away and saying the most beautiful words my ears have ever heard.

"Hello, baby. I'm your daddy."

Words haven't been invented yet to describe Tanner's voice as he speaks. It's a cross between melodious and reverent, but ultimately joyous. Like he's been waiting a lifetime to say those words. The events of the last three years leading up until today have felt like more than a lifetime. I know they have for me.

His luminous green eyes meet mine and I see the moisture beginning to well. This man on his knees before me, talking to our unborn child, is something I thought I'd never have. We've been through so much and each time my dreaded period came the last two months, I thought it was God's way of saying he didn't have plans for us to be parents. I know some people try for years to conceive a child but after losing Daniel, all I could think was that we'd never have that chance again.

But this moment right here, right now, has most definitely been worth the wait. Tanner's looking at me like I just hung the damn moon. I couldn't feel more loved if he tried.

"I have to have you," he says as he stands and pulls my naked body flush against his. His voice is almost as strained as the boxers he threw on when he got out of bed.

"You have me, always," I reply, my own tears seeping from my eyes.

My face bracketed between his hands, he uses his thumbs to wipe the wetness from my cheeks before lowering his lips to mine, rendering me breathless as he pours every emotion he's feeling into this kiss. Happiness, adoration and unconditional love. I'm a puddle of mush in his strong, loving arms.

Gliding his hands down my sides and sliding them around to cup my ass, he picks me up and heads for the bedroom. I have no choice but to wrap my legs around his lean, sculpted hips and hang on for what I'm sure will be an explosive ride.

Tanner deposits me in the middle of the bed, stands back to remove his boxers and lets his eyes roam my entire body. Having lost my shyness with him years ago, I let him look his fill, knowing damn well Tanner's a very visual man. Looking's half the fun for him. We've come a long way since the beginning of our relationship and I know just how happy losing my inhibitions makes him, which in turn makes me the most confident woman in the world with him, scars and all.

I look until my heart is content as well. How can any woman with a pulse not look at the marvel that is my husband? From the top of his head to the tips of his toes, he is perfectly perfect. Everything about him is perfect. His now slightly longer light brown hair, which is just the right length for me to run my hands through. His beautiful green eyes and strong square jaw. His broad muscular shoulders. His lickable, extremely defined eight pack, because six just wouldn't be enough for Tanner. That oh so yummy "V" that makes the entire female population stupid. And that cock. The cock he uses to do unspeakable things to my body. The cock that causes me to unconsciously lick my lips in anticipation.

"I can hear the dirty thoughts running through your mind, my sweet, dirty wife," he smiles down at me as he climbs on the bed and looms over me.

"I need you," I tell him spreading my legs to allow him room to slide between them.

"I know you do, I can see just how wet you are for me." And now I'm soaked. He takes one long digit and drags it through my slit, top to bottom, eliciting a moan that escapes my mouth before I realize it's happening.

"You like that, Ashley?" he asks with a knowing gleam in his eye. He knows damn well I love it but gets off on hearing the words leave my mouth.

"You know I do, husband," I can play this game just as good as he can. I know what calling him husband does to him. The first time I called him that, the night we were married, he took me so savagely I didn't think I'd be able to walk for a week. But good lord that was one of the best nights we've had together.

As predicted, his pupils dilate and he growls. Yes, growls. "I know what you're trying to do, but it's not going to work today, baby. Now's not the time for a good fucking. It's time for me to make love to my pregnant wife. It's time to worship you as you should be worshiped."

Christ, the shit that leaves this man's mouth should be downright illegal. I wish I could bottle it and sell it as some kind of foreplay enhancer. I'd make a freaking fortune.

Tanner's lips start their sensual assault with the spot behind my ear that always gets the party started. He licks and nibbles my earlobe before descending down my neck, peppering it with light, feather-like kisses. When he reaches the valley between my breasts, he plants one kiss in the middle before swirling his tongue around one of my nipples and ultimately pulling it into his mouth. He sucks before biting it gently, causing my back to arch up off the bed seeking more. But he doesn't grant me more, he just moves over to my other nipple giving it the same treatment.

"Please," I say, more than ready to have him inside me. Craving it.

"Not yet," he says continuing his descent down my body. He stops to pay homage to my scars from the accident. It used to make me uneasy until Tanner told me the scars make him appreciate that I'm still here and we still have a chance at this life we're creating. When he puts it like that, who am I to deny him?

By the time his lips make contact with my very wet core, I'm more than primed for the orgasm that will without a doubt rock my entire body.

Chapter Two

TANNER

I **DON'T EVEN** get my tongue inside Ashley's beautiful pussy before she's ready to blow. I thrust my tongue inside her once, twice and then she's screaming my name as she flies off the bed.

"Let me hear you, baby," I encourage her. "I love it when you're loud."

She moans loudly as I slide into her slowly, only giving her one inch at a time. "Fuck," she says as I thrust my remaining length inside her. I still myself and enjoy being balls deep in the love of my life. There's no greater place in the world than right here. I feel the aftershocks of her orgasm as her pussy weakly clenches and unclenches around me.

"Damn, there's nothing I love more than feeling you wrapped around my cock. This pussy was made just for me," I whisper in her ear as I pull myself out completely before thrusting back inside with the same slow pace as before. Her hips thrust up, encouraging me to go faster, but clearly, she didn't get the memo that I plan on enjoying everything her body has to offer… slowly.

Ashley's had a one track mind lately when it comes to sex. I almost feel as if she's been thinking of it as a job. It was always best to do it at this time, or in this position. I honestly wouldn't have been surprised if she told me I had to make love to her while she was hanging upside down from the damn ceiling. It was just about trying to get pregnant and not about us as a couple. But now, it's time to teach her to enjoy it again with no pressure.

"You're already pregnant, baby. No more clinical sex bullshit, now it's about us. Now we can just enjoy each other and have fun. You probably don't even remember what that is like, but I'm going to remind you. You're not calling the shots. Not anymore. You'll get what I give you and you'll fucking love it. I'm in control, again. Now lay back." I make sure to keep my eyes locked onto hers while I pick up the pace slightly, getting lost in the feel of Ashley's warm body. She does as she's told and as soon as she gives in to me, so does her body. The eye contact doesn't last much longer as Ashley moans, her body starting to spasm, and she closes her eyes. Nope, not today. Today, my wife will look into my eyes as she comes.

"Open those beautiful baby blues, baby. It's me I want you to see when you come. It will be me you see when you finally let go." Her eyes snap to mine and a smile slowly creeps across her face.

"It's you I always see when I come," she says breathlessly as her body shakes in extreme pleasure.

Her words are some of the most amazing she's ever said to me. Hearing them escape her lips as she's about to come apart pushes me to the edge. As I slide deep inside her, her pussy squeezes my cock and I can't hold back any longer. Resting my head on her shoulder, I let go and just let the wave take me over. Maybe it's because Ashley's pregnant. Maybe it's her words or the love pouring from her eyes. Maybe it's because sex with my wife is just that fucking amazing. Whatever it is, I just had the best orgasm of my life.

I lay here utterly content with my wife burrowed into my body as if she can't get close enough. I rest my chin on her head as I stare out the window, thinking about how perfect life can really be. I sigh and squeeze Ashley closer to me as I catch a glimpse of the leaves falling from the trees. The circle of life is an amazing thing. The miracle of life I've created with Ashley is amazing.

"I love you," Ashley says as she runs her fingers through my now sweaty hair.

"Not nearly as much as I love you," I tell her pulling my head back from hers so I can place a kiss on her lips. I don't stop at just her lips. I place kisses down the middle of her body until I get to her belly.

"Hi, little one. It's daddy. I can't wait to meet you. Until then, though, you hang out in there and be easy on Mommy, okay? I love you." *Nothing will ever hurt you.* Not just during these next nine months, but I will make it my life's mission to ensure that nothing hurts my child ever again.

Chapter Three

ASHLEY

HEADING INTO THIS appointment is a completely different experience from my first prenatal appointment with Daniel. Today I have Tanner by my side. My heart swells with love just looking at him, grinning from ear to ear.

As soon as the home pregnancy test came back positive, both Tanner and I wanted to get into the doctor right away. But Tanner had to travel to Oakland for a game last week and he was not going to miss this appointment, so we scheduled it for this week.

I've been an anxious mess waiting to get in here and see my little bean on the screen. I need to see him. Or her. I need the reassurance of seeing and hearing the heartbeat. My mind has been racing since finding out a few weeks ago. I'm terrified. For different reasons this time than the last. Last time I was in this position, I was terrified of doing it alone and being a single mother. I wasn't privy to how cruel the universe could be. Now, I'm scared of the unknown. Not just the unknowns of parenting but the unknown of the future. Will everything be okay this time around? Or will I have everything ripped from me again? I don't think this feeling will fade until I have the sweet little bundle in my arms. The only plus side now is that I have Tanner who will be here every step of the way with me.

Tanner must sense my anxiety because he plucks my hand out my lap and wraps his strong hand around it and places it in his lap instead. He leans over and places a kiss on my temple while giving my hand a reassuring squeeze. I smile at him just as the nurse emerges into the waiting room and calls my name.

"Mrs. Garrison."

I can feel the eyes of the other women in the room look over at me before I see it. The envy in their eyes is clear as day. I see it all the time. Women look at me and wish they could be on Tanner's arm. All they see is the extremely gorgeous NFL quarterback, with all the money and fame and privilege. I've never cared about any of that. All I want is him. We could be flat broke, living paycheck to paycheck and I'd still be happy.

Tanner rises from his chair pulling me along with him as he practically sprints to the door the nurse is standing at.

"Pleasure to see you again." She is one of the same nurses that was here when I was pregnant with Daniel, but I can't seem to remember her name.

"Thank you. You too." I smile politely.

"So glad you could make it today, Mr. Garrison," she says smiling at Tanner.

"I wouldn't miss it for the world," he says with a smile directed at me.

The nurse, whose name I remember is Lacey thanks to her name tag, gives me the run-down on the way to the exam room. After asking all her questions, she hands me the paper cup, gown, and tells me that Dr. Marcus will be in soon.

When I come out of the bathroom, I find Tanner checking out all the various things laying around the room. They have an exam kit on the counter and Tanner is checking out the contents of the package. I start to change out of my clothing while I silently laugh at Tanner's inspection of gynecological tools. He turns around when he hears the rustling of my pink paper gown as I slip my arms through it.

"What the hell do they do with this and why are your tits showing through that thing?" he asks holding the package pointing to the plastic speculum while staring at my boobs.

I can't hold back my laugh any longer. His face is so horrified it's hysterical. But I'm secretly glad he's never been to gyno's office with anyone else. "It's what they use to open your vagina for exams and my tits aren't showing anymore," I say as I wrap the gown around me.

His eyes are huge, round saucers and his jaw is clenched so hard I can see the muscles bulging under his ears. "You mean they're going to stick that inside you?" He's horrified. "And I'm just supposed to watch and be okay with another man inserting something into my wife's, you know?" He's dead serious which makes this even more comical.

"My 'you know'? For someone so practiced with dirty talk you use the words 'you know' in reference to my vagina?" I laugh at him.

"Ashley, this doesn't seem like the proper place to say pussy, know what I mean?" He whispers pussy like it's a secret word no one else can hear. "But that's not the important matter at hand here, is it? You expect me to watch a man stick something inside your… pussy and just watch like it's the most normal thing in the world? And I can still see your boobs through the arm holes."

"You realize that he looks at vaginas all day long. It's a job to him, Tanner, not a peep show and he's going to get a full view of my boobs when he does the breast exam." I'm hoping he can be rational about this. But if the roles were reversed, I wouldn't be too happy while he had a female doctor examining his junk.

"Fucking Christ…this just keeps getting better. I don't give a shit about all the other pussies he looks at. That is my pussy. And those are my tits." He says, anger still evident in his voice and all qualms about saying pussy here gone.

"You act like he's going to play with it," I laugh not being able to help taunting him. At least this whole ordeal is helping distract me from my nerves.

"Do. Not. Talk. About. Another. Man. Playing. With. My. Pussy." He snarls as the veins in his neck throb. *Okay, maybe taunting him wasn't a good idea.*

"I'm sorry, but you're going to have to get used to it if you want to come to these appointments. Otherwise, you're going to have to wait in the waiting room."

"I'm not waiting in the waiting room. Not an option," he snaps.

"Then stop being such an overbearing oaf. This is supposed to be a happy experience and you're turning into a jealous monster because the doctor has to see my vag and feel my boobs. That's the part of the body that the baby comes from. Nothing I can do about it, so you'll just have to deal." I demand, annoyed with this whole ridiculous standoff.

"Can't you have a woman doctor?" he asks sheepishly. I can tell he's still upset, but my threats to kick him out have him dialing it down.

"No. I like my doctor and I'm not switching. Deal with it. You'll be here the whole time, so you'll see there's nothing to worry about." That's where the conversation ends because Dr. Marcus strolls into the room completely unaware of my husband's extreme displeasure in this whole situation.

"Ashley. Tanner. Congratulations." He says extending his hand to shake Tanner's and smiles at me.

"Thank you," I smile back.

"According to your last period, you're due July 15th. A summer baby." He informs me as he picks up the strip the nurse dipped into the cup earlier. Holding it up, he says, "Yup. It's positive."

After ten minutes of questions, Dr. Marcus starts his pelvic exam and I think Tanner may actually have a coronary. He's quickly distracted though when Dr. Marcus says, "How about we see if we can get a good look at this little one?"

I shake my head vigorously since this is what I've been waiting for.

I fight back the laugh threatening to escape when Dr. Marcus grabs the ultrasound probe and covers it with a condom. Tanner looks like he's ready to kill someone or pass out. I'm not sure which. When the probe disappears under the paper covering draped over my legs, Tanner levels me with a hard stare and a very red face that lets me know he is in no way happy about what is happening at the moment.

His anger is short-lived, though. As soon as the screen displays black and white images of our little bean, Tanner squeezes my hand and stares at the image enraptured. His face has now softened and the huge cloud of tension has left replaced by joy and excitement. The fact that another man is between my legs seemingly forgotten.

"This white area right here…" Dr. Marcus says pointing to the area on the screen, "…is your baby."

He clicks and types on the keyboard of the ultrasound machine but all I can focus on is the image of our child on the screen and Tanner's face as he takes in what he's seeing for the first time. I can practically hear the thoughts running through his mind. We created this little life. A product of our love. A product of the long journey to the here and now. The unconditional love is pouring from his eyes for the baby and it melts my heart.

Dr. Marcus clicks a button on the machine and a loud whooshing sound overtakes the room. The echoing consumes the room. The sound of a new life being formed.

"Is that…" Tanner asks, still completely enthralled with the image being displayed for us. He hasn't taken his eyes off the screen. I can't say I blame him. I know how he feels. Seeing an image of your unborn child for the first time isn't something to take lightly. I can't form any words that would adequately explain how seeing this for the first time, with Tanner, makes me feel. Loved? Treasured? Fortunate? None of those seems to fit the bill.

I nod in answer to his question, unable to speak over the ball of emotion lodged in my throat.

"That's the most amazing sound I've ever heard," he utters in amazement.

"Yes. Yes, it is," I agree, a few tears escaping down my cheek.

Wiping them away with his thumb, Tanner leans down, his own tears streaking his face, "God, I love you so much. Thank you for this beautiful gift."

Chapter Four

TANNER

AFTER OUR FIRST appointment, Ashley and I decided that we weren't ready to share our news with everyone right away. We needed to enjoy our bliss between just the two of us before we shared it with the important people in our lives. To relish in our new found joy together, in ways we didn't get to the last time. I've made it my personal mission to have everything about this pregnancy be nothing but happy times for Ashley to reflect back on. Not that we want to forget our struggles with Daniel because it reminds me every day that we—I— have so much to be thankful for. I just want Ashley to look back at this experience with nothing but positive memories. I will do everything in my power to make sure she's absolutely happy.

Which brings me to making sure my darling wife has the best birthday I can give her. I decided last night while Ashley was curled around me that I would give her the best wake up I could think of. An orgasm high. The sigh of satisfaction that passes her lips, while I wipe her juices from my mouth on her inner thigh, tells me that she's pretty damn happy this morning!

"Have I told you lately how much I love it when I wake up with your head between my legs?" she giggles. I fucking love that sound, and the fact I can make my wife this happy, first thing in the morning.

"Happy Birthday, baby. I figured you'd like that better than breakfast in bed. So I had my breakfast in bed, instead." I say making my way up her body to kiss her mouth.

Wrapping her delicate fingers around my steel shaft, slowly stroking, "Do I get to have my breakfast now?" she asks.

"Well, I was planning on this just being about you, but far be it for me to deny the birthday girl anything she wants on her birthday. Have at it, baby," I say rolling over on my back.

Twenty minutes and a fewer brain cells later, I've made sure to clean up the mess I made on Ashley and slap her ass before kicking her out of the shower, "Let's go before I'm tempted to take you against the shower wall. I want to give you my present before I head down to the field."

"Ohh! More presents? You mean the delightful orgasm wasn't it?" she smiles facetiously.

"Well, I can take it back if that's all you wanted?" I smirk.

"Don't you dare! Where is it?" she asks, bouncing up and down like a little kid.

"Downstairs, in my office. Go get some clothes on and I'll give it to you."

"Why are you demanding clothing? It's always been optional before?" She's pushing her luck today.

"Because I need to be at the field soon and if you don't cover up that delectable body of yours, I'm going to be fined for being late. What I'd love to do to your body right now would not be quick." I give her my 'I mean business' stare, but she just drops her towel and prances to the closet like the little temptress she is. She's going to get it after her birthday dinner tonight.

AFTER PICKING OUT the skimpiest outfit I've ever seen someone wear in December—silk shorts and a tiny little top that I swear should be considered lingerie—she finally meets me in the kitchen. I hand her the box containing the most thoughtful gift I've ever come up with. And I did it all on my own. I spent hours designing it with the jeweler and I hope she loves it.

The room falls silent once she gets through the wrapping paper and opens the box. I'm actually getting nervous. Maybe I went all wrong with this gift. I should have just gotten her something ridiculous like a month long vacation in Europe.

"Oh, my god! It's stunning," she says finally breaking the silence and putting me out of my misery. "I love it."

"I'm glad," I say breathing a sigh of relief. I take the box from her hands and open the clasp so I can place the one of a kind charm bracelet on her wrist. "I told the designer what I wanted for each charm and he drew them up."

"I'd love for you to explain them to me," she smiles so brightly I'm sure she could melt the snow outside.

"Well, This one," I say pointing to the infinity symbol made entirely of small diamonds, "is a symbol of my love for you. There is no beginning and no end."

"And this one?" she asks pointing to the sapphire anchor.

"This one is a symbol of your strength and our strength together. You refuse to sink, even when the tide tries its hardest to pull you under. You always come out on top. Together there isn't anything we can't overcome. This one," I explain pointing to the heart shaped pendant. "is alexandrite. Pearl is the traditional stone for June, but pearls are so common. Alexandrite is a lesser known stone and you deserve something unique and rare, like our love, to symbolize the day

I made you my wife." This damn charm was a pain in my ass because a true piece of the gem is hard to find.

"This is the key to my heart. No one else has ever had it but you. And no one else ever will. And this one," I say before pointing to the last charm on the bracelet. "is to symbolize the beautiful future we have to look forward to. Not only that, but a compass symbolizes many things. It provides guidance and navigation through life's unexpected twists and turns. Each direction has a significant meaning. North represents home and infinite possibility. South embodies passion and the present. East signifies new beginnings and the future. West represents emotion and new beginnings."

She smiles, moisture evident in her eyes. "This is the most thoughtful gift I've ever been given. And not just because it's gorgeous. The thought you put into this means more to me than you could ever know."

"Happy Birthday, baby. I love you." I smile at the delight written all over her face. This is all I want for her. She deserves nothing but a lifetime of moments like this.

"I love you, too," she smiles back before wrapping herself around me and showing me her gratitude with a kiss so hot I'm more than willing to take the damn fine for being late to practice.

"Okay go before I drag you back to bed. Then you'll blame me for the coach being pissed and I'm not having any of that today," she says breaking our kiss. "What time do I need to be ready for dinner?"

"Six. We're going to meet everyone there at six-thirty." I've planned a small dinner with my family and Quinn for later tonight.

"Okay. Have a good day at practice. I'm meeting Quinn at the spa in an hour."

"No saunas and make sure they don't use any oils on you. No chemical peels or anything either," I remind her. I've read all the damn books and get daily emails about pregnancy from every pregnancy website you can think of. One last week happened to be all about spa safety during pregnancy. It's a toss-up between who's being more cautious with the pregnancy warnings of not doing this or that.

"I will. I'm just getting a facial, massage and mani-pedi. Nothing crazy, I promise," she smirks at my worry, but I know she secretly loves it.

"Have fun. See you later."

Chapter Five

ASHLEY

"**SORRY, I'M LATE,**" Quinn apologizes as she rushes through the entrance of the spa.

"It's okay, I haven't been waiting long," I tell her as I watch her take off her coat and hang it on the coat rack. I'm surprised by her too-casual-for-Quinn-in-public appearance. Quinn is always decked out to the nines no matter what she's doing. Seeing her dressed in a casual long sleeve tunic paired with leggings and Uggs is a pretty rare occurrence.

"You know how hard it is getting appointments in this place, but my mother didn't seem to care. She decided to drop by this morning to do my father's bidding," she huffs angrily. "Why don't they understand that I don't give a shit about their quest to be one of the wealthiest families in New York?"

"They really want this to go through, huh? Still not getting that you want no part?" I ask still trying to get over my shock of her casualness.

This battle with her parents must really be bothering her for Quinn to leave the house like this.

"Yes, and they just don't understand that I don't want what they have. Mother will do whatever father tells her to, thus proving my point even further. How can she be happy with that life? I don't get it. Which is why I don't want it. How can they just expect me to be okay with this and go along with it like it's what I want?" I'm worried she's about to lose it. She's pacing the small entrance area mumbling obscenities to herself, something she only does when she's pushed to her limit. Usually, she'll shout them from the rooftop for everyone to hear. I haven't ever really seen Quinn this bothered by something, with the exception of me after the accident.

"I know you have a ton of shit going on, but let's just try to enjoy the day. We have a full morning of pampering ahead of us, so ignore all this drama for a few hours and have a good time. We're not letting your parents ruin our girl time here. Do you know how hard it is to get into this place?" I smirk, repeating her earlier words back to her before checking us in with the receptionist, who has been giving us a look of disdain since Quinn walked through the door. If she wasn't so distracted, she would've already ripped this chick a new one.

"Please have a seat through the door, someone will come collect you when your rooms are ready," the bitch behind the desk says as she directs us to the relaxation room, with a wave of her hand.

"So what did Superstar get you for your birthday?" Quinn asks as we settle into the overstuffed white leather couch in the relaxation area.

"His best gift to date," I exclaim, waving my wrist which is now adorned with my new charm bracelet.

"Very nice. Why's it so special? It's just a charm bracelet?" she asks, her irritation and disgust with her parents still evident in the less than enthused tone of her voice. I can't really blame her, I know how much their pushiness with this bullshit has been bothering her lately.

"He had it specially designed and each charm has a special meaning," I explain smiling down at my wrist.

"Aww, that's sweet," she smiles at me as she grabs a magazine off of the coffee table in front of us. It's not a real smile. It's her romance is bullshit smile and I'm lying through my teeth right now because I don't see the signification of the song and dance of love. I can't tell you how many times I've seen that smile over the years. Mostly during college when our sorority sisters would come bragging about this gift or what so and so said they would do after graduation. "Another mindless drone of love" Quinn would say to me as our sisters and friends all fell in love. Quinn just doesn't believe in love.

"You're hopeless," I huff, calling her out on her condescending comment, just as the assistant comes out to tell us that our room is ready. It's as if she thought she was going to be able to give me the fake shit she always gives everyone else. As if I wouldn't notice. But I know how difficult her parents have been making this on her so I'll cut her a little slack for now.

"I've never claimed to be fixable, sweets," she reminds me as we head back to spend the next few hours in girly bliss.

TWO AND A half hours later I've been waxed, rubbed, scrubbed, filed and polished and I feel amazing!

"I think that's just what I needed," Quinn says with a smile as we head out to the parking lot. "I feel like a whole new woman."

"Mmm… Me too." I agree. "So I'll see you tonight at six-thirty?"

"Of course. I wouldn't miss this dinner for the world," she smiles at me. There's still a hint of sadness and frustration in her voice, but she's volumes better than when she arrived.

"YOU SURE YOU want to tell them tonight?" Tanner asks as we make our way into Dino and Harrison's, our usual spot for dining out. The owners always allow for us to use their back room and do what they can to allow for our privacy while we're here. It's pretty hard to stay inconspicuous in this area during football season. Before Tanner, the Jets haven't had a winning season in fifty years. With one Super Bowl and making it to two AFC Championships in three years, everyone has Tanner fever. We can't go anywhere without getting mobbed. It's exciting, but it gets old quickly. Sometimes we just want to go out for a quiet dinner like normal people.

"Why wouldn't I?" I question, confused as to why he doesn't want to share our news.

"Well, it's your birthday. I thought that maybe you'd just want today to be about celebrating you," he explains as he holds open the door for me.

"You know I'm not that girl," I chide him. "I can't think of a better thing to celebrate on my birthday other than our little miracle," I smile at him as we walk in. Recognizing us right away, the hostess motions for us to follow her to the private room in the back.

"I know you're not, but I just wanted to make sure you're okay with this. Once we tell my mom and sisters, they're going to go crazy. Are you prepared for that tonight?" he points out.

He's right, everyone will go bananas. "I'm ready."

"Okay then, in you go," he says opening the next door.

We spend the next twenty minutes greeting everyone—Tanner's parents, his sisters and their families and Quinn.

"Ashley are your parents coming tonight?" Beth, one of Tanner's sisters, asks.

"No, we're not on the best of terms right now." I would've loved to invite my father, but I know he wouldn't come unless I extended the invitation to my mother, and there's no way in hell that was going to happen.

I'm saved from having to go any further into the horrors of my relationship with my mother by the waiter, Michael. He's the same waiter that we have every time we come here. We know that Tanner's used dinner napkin isn't going to wind up on EBay with him.

He drops off a glass of champagne in front of everyone and then asks for our appetizer orders.

"Would you like your usual shucked oyster platter for an appetizer today, Mr. and Mrs. Garrison?" he asks once he gets to our side of the table.

"No, not today Michael. I'd really love some mozzarella sticks, though," I say suddenly craving fried grease and marinara sauce.

"Sure, no problem," he says as he writes my order down on his pad. I notice the funny look he gives me. He's not the only one. Everyone is kind of looking at me funny. It is weird for me to pass up oysters here, though. I'm always raving about them. I'm going to miss them over the next seven months.

Tanner clinks his knife against his glass as Michael retreats to the kitchen with the orders for our first course. "I'd like to make a toast."

Everyone raises their glasses while I just stare at the handsome profile of my wonderful husband, "To my beautiful wife, Ashley. Happy Birthday, baby! I hope it's your best year yet. I love you."

I grab my glass of water and clink my glass with his as a round of Salutes echo around us.

I catch a glimpse of Margaret as I make my way around the table "cheers-ing" with everyone. She glances down at my belly then to the water in my hand and a small smile creeps along her face. She's not a dumb woman. I can see the wheels spinning in her head as she's putting two and two together. I just hope she doesn't say anything just yet.

"So what did Tanner get you for your birthday?" Veronica, Tanner's oldest sister, asks pulling my attention away from Tanner's mother.

"Well," I start as I reach across the table to grab a breadstick from the basket. "This is one of them," I say shaking my wrist, loving the sounds my bracelet makes.

As his sisters and mom 'ooh' and 'ahh' over the bracelet, I glance at Tanner and see him giving me a quizzical look, clearly wondering what the other gift I'm talking about could be since he only gave me the bracelet as a present this morning. I just wink at him.

"What else did you get?" Beth inquires.

"Yeah, what else did you get?" Quinn chimes in clearly wondering what I didn't share with her earlier today.

"Well, the other was an early birthday he gave me about two months ago," I give away to see if anyone other than Margaret has been paying close enough attention tonight to pick up on the other hints.

Having confirmed her earlier suspicions, Margaret pushes her chair back, walks around the table and wraps me in a hug. She rests her hand on my belly for a brief moment, but not everyone can see her do it from our positions. Just Tanner, his dad and his niece who is sitting next to him.

"What's going on, Ma?" Veronica asks, clearly not happy about being on the outside of this.

"Yeah, what Ma?" Beth adds clearly confused as well.

"No fucking way. It took me a minute, but I get it now," Quinn says, pushing her chair back and rounding the table to hug me as well. "I'm so fucking happy for you."

"Quinn!" Veronica and Beth both chastise her use of language by nodding toward Tanner's two nieces and nephew.

"Sorry, guess I better work on that. Especially with another one on the way," she smiles at me.

"Holy shit," both sisters gasp together.

"Ha, who gets to yell at you now?" Quinn laughs at their shock.

"Are you going to have a baby, Aunt Ashley?" Maci, Veronica's ten-year-old daughter asks.

"Yes, sweetie, I am," I smile at her before taking in the overjoyed faces around the room. Best birthday ever.

As Tanner predicted we were bombarded with questions about the baby but ultimately everyone was overjoyed with our news.

We spend the rest of dinner talking about babies. Tanner's sisters telling me everything I need to do to get ready. And then they proceeded to tell me every gross thing about childbirth, stretch marks and the joys of engorged breasts. Quinn effectively ended that whole topic of conversation by promising to tell the kids how babies are really made if Veronica and Beth didn't shut the hell up. Having known Quinn long enough to know she wasn't kidding, they shut up.

Everyone places bets if the baby will be a boy or a girl and then gives their ideas for names. Finally, after eating way too much birthday cake, we call it a night. "Did you have a good birthday, baby?" Tanner prods as we pull in the garage.

"It was fantastic. I wish Alex was here, though. We'll have to call him with the news before word spreads," I frown. Even after a year and a half of him being in Arizona, I still get bummed when he misses the big things. When he was offered the job as the head trainer for the Cardinals, I didn't really think he'd take it. Tanner said their offer was just too good for him to turn down.

"I know, me too." He agrees. "I don't want to tell him over the phone, though, so maybe we'll just have to Skype or FaceTime him. I don't want to wait until after the season to tell him in person." I completely agree with him. It's not fair to wait until the end of the season to tell him, but a phone just won't do.

I look at my watch. "We can do it tonight if you want. It's still early over there," I offer.

"That could work," Tanner sighs. Things were so much easier when both our closest friends were on the same side of the country. Not that it really matters anymore since they can't seem to be in the same room together—let alone actually speaking to one another.

Chapter Six

ASHLEY

THE GARRISON FAMILY has had an away game ritual for the last three seasons. We all gather at my house and watch the game together. Some of my favorite times have happened on these Sundays. Of course, I always miss Tanner but all of us huddle together on the sofas in the screening room and stare at a very hot HD version of Tanner.

The first time we had this get-together, I tried to cook appetizers for everyone. This is how the whole family came to know I can't cook for shit. What I didn't burn tasted like dog food so needless to say, we wound up ordering pizza that day.

We've evolved from just pizza now. Andrew, Tanner's dad, makes his delicious chili. Margaret always brings a pan of lasagna and platter of meatballs. Beth, the baker of the family, as always brings brownies, cookies, and cupcakes for the kids. Veronica has been in charge of wings because you can't watch a game without wings. I order the pizza, get the chips and stock the beer. Twice a month, during the season, we have these gatherings and we all love them.

The Jets have the potential to clinch their division if they win their next two games against the Patriots and Bills. Selfishly, I hope they do. I could use an extra week with Tanner before the chaos of the playoffs.

"Kick off in two minutes," Tony, Veronica's husband, yells from the screening room.

"We better get moving then," Margaret says grabbing a bowl of chips. Beth and Veronica each grab a bowl of snacks while I grab a bottle of orange juice for myself. Last time, I forgot that we only had beer in the refrigerator in the screening room. I had to run back to the kitchen when I wanted a drink and I missed a forty-yard pass by Tanner.

This is going to be an interesting game. There's a big rivalry between the Jets and the Patriots. If you're a Jets fan, you most likely hate the Pats and vice versa. No one is expecting a warm reception for our boys in Massachusetts today.

It's obvious within the first five minutes of the game that both sides came to play and play hard. There's no mercy being shown on either side of the ball. These boys are fighting for each yard. The Pats defense calls a blitz and I see the linebackers gun it for Tanner. I want to close my eyes. I don't want to see these men run full speed into my husband and lay him on his ass. But if I close my eyes I might miss a good play, so I force myself to keep them open.

With a move you only see in movies about football, Tanner sidesteps one massive guard charging at him and ducks under the other, which causes the linebacker to roll over Tanner's back. He manages to scramble to the left. He finds a man open downfield. The balls leaves Tanner's hand in a perfect spiral and hits the tight end's hands with amazing accuracy as he falls into the end zone.

We all jump up and scream! High fives are flying between everyone and hugs are going around.

After hugging her husband, Dillion, Beth comes back to her seat next to me on the sofa. Her smile drops as she looks at me with a horrified expression. "Ashley, don't move." Her eyes dart from me to my ass and then back again.

"Oh dear," I hear Margaret gasp and then everyone starts talking at once. I still haven't moved a muscle and have no idea what all the ruckus is about.

"What the hell is going on?" I yell over the commotion. The room goes silent and everyone just stares at me. The game unfolding on the TV completely forgotten.

Margaret steps closer to me and puts her hand on my shoulder before speaking, "There's blood on your pants, dear."

It takes me a minute to figure why everyone is making a big deal about the fact that I sat in something until it clicks that Margaret said blood and the fear settles in like a lead balloon.

"No. No. No." I shake my head as if that will make the situation go away. My hands move to cradle my belly which hasn't even started to pop yet.

"Just relax, sweetie," Veronica says. "Why don't you go to the bathroom and see how bad it is and we'll get the doctor on the phone for you."

THE LAST TWENTY minutes are a huge blur in my mind. I'm now sitting in the passenger seat of my car with Margaret driving me to the hospital. Dr. Marcus informed Veronica to have me head down to the hospital but remain calm, it's probably nothing. Easy for him to say. I bet he never started a day with a healthy pregnancy only to have it end the complete opposite. *Twice.*

Grabbing my hand, Margaret gives it a reassuring squeeze. "Just relax, dear. I'm sure everything is fine."

We just announced last week that we're having this baby. We should've waited. We told everyone about it and jinxed it. The universe has changed its mind about me being a mother. I'm paying back some serious Karma. Couldn't I have just not been able to conceive? That would have been easier to deal with. Who have I made so mad that I have to endure the loss of another child? *Alone.*

My husband is in the middle of a football game three states away and has no idea what is going on. This is some serious déjà vu. "I need to call Tanner."

"Tony sent him a text telling him to call one of us immediately after he reads it. Just relax and stay calm. Everyone is making sure everything is covered. You just need to focus on trying to stay calm. I know how hard that is right now, but that baby needs you to stay comfortable and composed. Stress isn't going help." She squeezes my hand again and I try to allow my body to release the tension. Margaret is right. Stress won't help. I have a huge family that's taking care of everything. My only concern right now should be the baby.

We pull up to the valet, then after getting our ticket, we head into the emergency department of the hospital.

"May I help you?" The clerk behind the desk asks as we approach.

"Yes, Ashley Garrison. My doctor is expecting me." My voice is shaking, the fear evident.

The man behind the desk types on his keyboard and clicks a few different things before confirming, "Dr. Marcus is waiting for you upstairs. Take those elevators over there up to the fifth floor."

"Thank you." I hear Margaret answer. Her voice is distant since I'm already making my way to the elevator. I silently chide myself for being rude. It's not that man's fault I'm here.

Exiting the elevator, I'm greeted with a set of double doors that reads: *Labor and Delivery.* A small sign above an intercom reads: *Please buzz for entry.* After pressing the button, the sweet voice of a woman behind the doors answers. "May I help you?"

"Yes, Ashley Garrison."

I hear the click of the doors opening before she responds, "Come on in."

"Ashley," Dr. Marcus greets me. "I'm glad I'm the one here on-call today. Why don't we head into room four over here and see what's going on?"

I'm ushered into the room where I'm handed a gown and a cup. "You can leave the cup on the counter. I'll give you a few minutes and then I'll be back and we'll see what's going on. I'm sure everything is fine."

Dr. Marcus returns to the room with an ultrasound machine just as I'm settling into the bed.

"Have you had any cramping with the spotting Ashley?" he asks as he boots up the machine.

"No."

"Any pain?"

"No."

"I need you to pull your gown up so I can get to your belly, please," he says as he grabs the gel from the holder on the machine. "Has the spotting increased in flow?"

I shake my head as I watch him squirt the gel on my belly before placing the probe over it. It takes less than a minute before I hear the highly anticipated whooshing take over the room. I can't explain how the tears came so fast. But in this moment, I sob knowing my baby still has a heartbeat.

Margaret rubs her hand in circles on my shoulder, "Everything is just fine, dear."

Dr. Marcus nods in agreement. "I don't see anything alarming, Ashley. Spotting is fairly common in the first trimester. Heartbeat sounds strong."

"Everything was just fine the last time too," I point out. I don't think either of them fully grasps my fear of history repeating itself.

"If your abruption had been caused by high blood pressure or a genetic disorder, I'd say you have reason to be concerned. But yours was caused by an auto accident. Unless you suffer another trauma, you have no reason to be worried. But I do want you to take it easy for a few days," he explains as he wipes the gel from my belly.

"I'll have my son make sure she takes it easy," Margaret tells the doctor with relief clearly written on her face.

OUR RIDE HOME from the hospital is quiet. I'm still having a hard time believing nothing is going to go wrong. All I want right now is my husband. As if he senses my need for him, my phone starts blaring *Thinking Out Loud,* my ring tone for Tanner.

"Hello."

"Ashley, baby, what's going on? I just got Tony's message." His voice is panicked and frantic.

"I'm heading home from the hospital now…" I start to explain.

"Hospital? Why were you at the hospital? Is everything okay?" The inflection in his voice rises, as it does when he's really worried.

"There was some spotting so Dr. Marcus told me to head to the hospital to be checked out. Everything seems to be okay. I have to take it easy."

"How's the baby? Is everything okay with the baby, though? How did you get to the hospital? So help me god, you better not have driven yourself." He fires question after question without giving me a chance to answer.

"I'm with your mom. As of right now the doctor said that everything is ok. How long until you get home?" I really hope that he is already on the plane.

"Shouldn't be more than two hours or so," he answers sounding slightly winded as if he's rushing around. Which he probably is. I can tell by the fast pace of speech he's upset. Tanner tends to talk fast whenever he's distressed.

Knowing he's going to be home soon, I feel as though I can breathe again. "Okay. I'll see you when you get home. I'm just going to head up to bed when I get back."

"Is Ma going to stay with you?"

"I don't think so. There's no reason really. I'm just going to lay down and try and get some sleep while I wait for you." I want to be alone but I don't at the same time. There are a million things running through my mind right now. All different scenarios of how this plays out with the same ending as the last time I was pregnant. No baby and pure heartbreak. But I don't want Tanner to know that right now. Not when we are this far apart and he can't hold me.

I'VE BEEN DOZING on and off for the last hour or so when I hear Tanner heading up the stairs. Our bedroom door swings open and Tanner is on his knees at the side of the bed pulling my face to his. "I'm so sorry I wasn't here for you today, baby. Do you know how awful I felt knowing what you were going through here without me? I promised you I would be here every step of the way and I wasn't."

"It's not like you were out at a nightclub, Tanner. You were working and you're here now," I reply, leaning into his touch as if it alone is enough to keep all my fear at bay.

Tanner stands and undresses as he makes his way around the bed. He climbs in and pulls me into his body, cocooning me. "Tell me what happened."

I rehash the events of the day and tell him everything Dr. Marcus said. "How are you feeling about everything?"

I sigh and pull his arms tighter around me. "I'm scared. It's still early and we could still lose the baby at any time. I can't handle that. I know I can't. I don't think I'll feel good about anything until this little one is in my arms."

"Everything will be okay. I promise." If only he could guarantee that promise. If only.

Chapter Seven

TANNER

ASHLEY HASN'T DONE more than shower and move from one resting spot to another in over two weeks. She was terrified after the spotting incident, but the doctor has reassured us twice now that everything is ok. She called the next morning and asked if she could come in and make sure that everything was still okay. They fit her in that day and Dr. Marcus confirmed again everything was just fine. The heartbeat was strong and our little alien-looking baby was floating around in there healthy as can be.

We had another appointment last week, which was at Ashley's insistence, and again Dr. Marcus assured us the baby looked wonderful. He really has been amazing these two weeks with Ashley's fears, calling her back with an answer to every question she's had, adding the extra appointment to ease her worry. Hell, I was pretty fucking scared too but I started to let that fear slowly dissipate after our first follow up appointment.

I asked Dr. Marcus how long Ashley needed to be on bed rest. He informed me that he never actually put her on bed rest, which is exactly what she interpreted his orders of taking it easy to mean. He told her resuming all her daily activities was fine.

Normally, I have no problem with Ash doing nothing but relaxing. It's her fear of the unknown that has me worried. She doesn't do anything but read about miscarriages and possible causes of them. What she's doing to herself isn't healthy and it's bordering on obsessive. She's changed her diet and decided that the gym routine she usually does is too much for the baby. She's basically changed anything she could think of based on what she read online about possible causes of miscarriages. I love my wife, but her problem with relying on the information on the internet is driving me completely insane.

She has thrown out all of our cleaning supplies because the chemicals might endanger the baby. She's replaced them with an all-natural line, but even that she's cautious of. We even have new soap and shampoo that Ashley claims is the most organic product they have out, made purely from things found in nature. She insisted we have the house tested for mold, twice. When the first test came back negative, she called another company in 'just to be sure'. I tried to draw the line at letting her have the house tested for lead-based paint. The house is only eight years old. I tried, nicely, to point out that we didn't need to do that because they didn't use lead paint anymore when our house was built. She yelled at me claiming that I didn't care about the safety of the baby, so I let her schedule the stupid test. The guy who came out must have thought we were both morons for wanting a house built in 2008 to be tested for lead.

I've decided to take matters into my own hands and force her out of her safety net. The foundation is having its annual New Year's celebration and we're going. Ashley told me earlier this week she didn't think it was a good idea because walking around in heels could put too much strain on her back and she was supposed to be taking it easy. I'm seriously considering canceling our internet.

Quinn is having a few dresses couriered over here for Ashley to pick from. She's also having a slew of flat shoes sent over to match. No excuses from my darling wife today. I purposely waited for the day of the event so she couldn't research more reasons not to go. She needs to live her life and enjoy this experience.

Strolling into the bedroom, I find Ashley lying in her usual spot on the sofa at the far end of the room. Her computer in her lap. I know she's faking working and looking up more false information because the papers all around her are upside down. She's completely impossible.

"Hey baby," I smile. "Almost done with your article?"

I know I catch her off guard because she jumps. I know what she's about to say before the words even leave her mouth, "Jesus! You scared the hell out of me, Tanner. You know that's not good for the baby."

Christ, she's gone completely insane. "I didn't mean to. I wasn't exactly quiet on my way in here."

"It's okay, just give me more of a heads up next time other than heavy footsteps. As for work, I'm just going over all the notes I have for the articles I need to finish up." She tells me as she gathers up all the papers as if she's going to read them.

I walk over casually and grab the papers from her hands. "Hey, I was reading those."

"No, you weren't, unless you can read upside down now." I point out before continuing. "You're googling more stupid shit that can cause miscarriages."

"No I wasn't," she snaps crossing her arms over her chest. I don't say anything. I just raise an eyebrow at her calling her out on her lie, but she doesn't say anything.

"You are almost at the end of your first trimester. The chances of you miscarrying at twelve weeks are less than five percent. You need to stop obsessing."

"I'm not obsessing," she frowns. She doesn't understand why I don't feel the need to continuously worry that something bad is going to happen. Yes, of course, I'm worried a little bit that something could always go wrong, but in this situation, stress will only make things worse.

"You are, which is why we are going to the party tonight." She starts to say something, but I don't give her the chance. "You are. Dresses and shoes are being couriered over as we speak and I even had Quinn order a special line of organic make-up for you."

"But… I don't think it's a good idea. There will be lots of drunk people there tonight and what if someone bumps into me? The doctor said to avoid trauma." I see we are at a whole other level of extreme today.

"I assure you I will make sure that no one bumps into you tonight but even if that should happen, someone accidentally bumping into you isn't trauma, Ashley." I really don't know how to come out of this without looking like an asshole. I understand her fear, but she's being totally neurotic.

Kneeling down in front of her, I grab her hands and sigh, "I'm worried about you, baby. All the stress and tension you're carrying around aren't good for the baby either. You can't live in this bubble of fear. You're supposed to be enjoying this time. Relishing in the new life we've created. Excited for the future. Not frozen in fear. I miss you."

"But I'm scared," she whispers.

"It's ok to be scared, Ash, but what you are doing isn't healthy. You're reading a bunch of shit that doesn't necessarily have any merit to it. Any jackass with a keyboard can post something, but that doesn't make it reliable or accurate. Trust Dr. Marcus, he would never steer you wrong. Do you think going back to Dr. Patterson would help you?" I'm surprised that I didn't think of that suggestion earlier. After the accident, Dr. Patterson had the ability to help Ashley see reason.

A look of shock covers her face at my suggestion. "Do you think I've gotten so bad that I need to go back to therapy?"

Brushing a stray piece of hair behind her ear, I shake my head. "That's not what I'm saying, sweetheart. I'm just trying to find a way to help you work through your fears. I want to see you happy, having fun again, enjoying life instead of being afraid of it."

After a few moments of silence, she relents. "Okay. I guess I can loosen up a little. It's been two weeks and everything has been fine. And I'm really starting to hate the décor of our bedroom."

"That's my girl," I smile as I lean forward to kiss her.

I GIVE ASHLEY credit, she's really trying to have a good time tonight. I've stayed true to my words and haven't left her side. Which means I'm currently sitting at our table, being forced to listen to her and Quinn talk about the douche canoe Quinn came with tonight.

"He isn't bad looking," Ashley says as she snacks on some bread.

"Who cares? He's still a tool," Quinn snaps as she drains her glass of wine.

"Well, at least he's not awful to look at. It could be worse." Alright, I love my wife and I'm glad that she hasn't thought about anything that could harm the baby here in the last twenty minutes, but I can't sit around and listen to this girl babble.

"How about a dance?" I ask as I stand and button my suit jacket. I don't give Ashley a chance to answer before I grab her hand and pull her out of her chair.

Once we're on the dance floor, I spin my wife into me and smile at her as some Michael Buble song plays in the background. "Are you having a good time?"

"I am," she smiles. "I'm glad you forced me here. I didn't think I would enjoy myself, but I am. It's nice to get back into the world."

"I'm sorry if I came across as an ass, but I just can't stand to see you doing this to yourself. I understand your fears, but I missed seeing you be you." I want to make sure she knows I was a little rough on her out of love and not for any other reason.

"I guess I was going a little crazy, but I'm sticking with the diet and chemical-free stuff. That is still good for the baby."

I don't care if she wants to go vegan and live off of tofu. "That's fine, baby. I don't care about those changes. I just don't like you holed up in the house like the sky is going to fall if you walk outside."

Ashley doesn't make a move to leave the dance floor so I continue to twirl her across the floor, enjoying seeing some light on my wife's face for the first time in weeks. She's beautiful in every way on a regular day but when she's smiling and carefree, she's absolutely breathtaking.

I've been having such an amazing time watching my wife let her hair down, I didn't even realize it's almost midnight until Quinn shows up with her loser date. She hands a glass to each of us.

"Countdown bitches," Quinn sings out obviously a little tipsy.

Ashley bring her glass up and sniffs, "What's in my glass?"

"Sparkling cider, baby," Quinn says while twirling in a circle. Okay, she may be full blown drunk.

Everyone starts the countdown and on one I spin my wife around and plant my lips on hers. It was supposed to only be a sweet kiss, but it quickly turns into raw heat.

"You think you're up to heading home and spending some quality time together? I can help you with the whole relaxing thing." I waggle my eyebrows not expecting her to say yes but honestly hoping she does. I really miss connecting with her.

My jaw nearly hits the floor when she smirks at me and says, "Well, the doctor did say I could resume my regular activities right?"

"He sure did."

Tossing me a saucy look over her shoulder, she starts pulling me toward the door, “Then I guess you better resume your daily love making to your wife. You’ve been really slacking these last few weeks.”

Chapter Eight

ASHLEY

THE LAST TWO weeks have been a complete whirlwind. From the moment the Jets won the AFC championship things have been crazy! Interviews, press conferences, extended practices, life has been total chaos. While Tanner has been dealing with all the media hoopla, I've decided maybe a few sessions with Dr. Patterson wasn't a bad idea. I'm glad Tanner pointed out I might need her. I've felt a little lighter since speaking with her. I'm in a much better place. She reminded me that I can always come in for a few sessions here and there when I need help dealing with what life throws at me, especially with the anniversary of the accident right around the corner.

We've been in Atlanta for the last week and today is the big day! I thought the pressure leading up to the championship game was intense, but this is a whole new level of intense. Tanner's in the zone. This is such an exciting, but stressful, time. We're both struggling with the dark moments this event brings for us. It's the anniversary of the accident and losing Daniel. We're both trying to push it aside, but that hasn't been easy considering every dickhead with a microphone wants to probe into the worst times of our life. Reporters can't seem to get enough of the coincidence that I'm pregnant again during this time. Tanner has taken it all in stride; giving the scripted answers his PR people have told him to say.

Tanner's quiet and focused. Playful Tanner is gone. He has a single focus. Winning. It's really a site to see. He doesn't talk much and spends most of what little downtime he gets, watching film of Arizona's last two games. I'm so thankful Alex doesn't actually play so they won't be battling each other on the field.

There is so much nervous energy floating between us before he leaves for the stadium that it's stifling. "There will be mass pandemonium on the field if we win. Please don't take this the wrong way, but I don't want you down there if we do. I know families will be flocking down to the field, but I don't want you in that crazy of a crowd. I don't need anything to happen to you," he explains with a tone that expresses how much this is weighing on him. He doesn't need to remind me of our troubled luck with this event.

"Okay. I won't come down to the field," I concede. I don't want to argue with him right now, no matter how much I want to celebrate the win with my husband if the time comes. I understand where he's coming from though and I know it's not malicious.

"I want you in the locker room after everything settles down. Regardless," he commands. "It's going to take me a while to get there but make sure that my Dad escorts you down. I don't want you anywhere alone." For once I think he's the one going a little off the deep end here.

"Okay, I'll stay with your dad, but honestly, what do you think could happen to me in a place filled with that many people?" I ask. I don't understand where all this extremeness is coming from.

"Do you not remember when the 49ers won the Super Bowl in 2001 and a crazed fan murdered the quarterback's wife right on the field during an interview?" he asks as though he's completely appalled I'm not familiar with the tragedies of huge sporting events.

"Seriously?" I ask unable to believe that something so terrible could happen in such a public way.

"Yes. Aiden Aldrich was football royalty. His wife was America's sweetheart of tennis and it was all on national television." He explains realizing that I don't really have any clue about what he's talking about.

"How horrible. That poor family."

"Yeah, big events can bring all the crazies out of the woodwork. Understand why you aren't to go off on your own now?" he questions reiterating his earlier point.

"Yes, I won't go anywhere alone." I nod, repeating my earlier words but with more understanding.

"The suite there will be the usual set-up, as always, so anything you want, just ring for it," he explains as he makes his way to grab his duffle by the hotel door.

"Okay. Good luck. I love you, either way, Superstar," I smile as I follow him to the door.

"Love you, too." And he's gone.

TANNER'S FAMILY, QUINN and I pull up to the Georgia Dome and its crazy packed. Fans everywhere. Every inch of the parking lot is covered with people tailgating. I'm so glad we get to go through the private entrance; a crowd that size is not something I want to deal with right now.

We exit the town car, which Tanner arranged for us. There's security everywhere.

"Can I help you?" A large imposing man asks as we near the entrance.

We flash our passes and are allowed to enter.

"Wow," we all gasp at the same time.

I was a little sad when Tanner told me that I wouldn't get to see him until the game. But now I'm glad that I wasn't allowed to come with him earlier. I wouldn't have been able to sit around all day with the chaos that is going on here.

We're guided to the owner's box. You'd think there was a wedding happening in here. There are tables along one side of the suite loaded with food and beverages. I can't believe how all out they go. We all mill about for a little bit and settle in while things stir up down on the field.

"Holy shit! This is so intense," I whisper to Quinn as the National Anthem starts blaring from all the speakers. I couldn't even tell you who is singing it because I'm so fucking nervous. And I'm not even out on the field.

"I know. It's fucking insane in here," she whispers back, nodding her head down toward the field.

I wish I could say the feeling settled, but by the end of the first half, I'm even more of a fucking wreck. The Jets are down fourteen to seven, and I seriously can't take all this anxiety.

"Relax, Ashley, There's still a whole half of the game to play," Andrew reminds me as he rubs circles on my back. "You've sure come a long way from the girl who couldn't tell the difference between a first down and a touchdown," he laughs.

"Yes, dear, you're too worked up," Margaret says agreeing with Andrew.

"I wish I could have a shot or two right now," I exhale.

"I'll have a few for you, sweets. I'm more than happy to take one for the team," Quinn tells me with a huge grin. God, I miss that smile. Today is the happiest I've seen her in a long time.

"So thoughtful of you," I roll my eyes at her.

"Let's get some food," Tanner's sister, Veronica, says. "This shit is going to most likely last another twenty minutes and my ears can't take it." I laugh. She's right. The chick performing the halftime show can't sing for shit and it sounds terrible. She's obviously auto-tuned while recording and doesn't have the talent to perform live.

"Food sounds like a good distraction," I nod at Veronica and join her at the table set up near the entrance of the suite.

A full belly, bleeding ears and twenty minutes later, we are back in our seats waiting for the kickoff of the second half. Too bad it's not any easier to stomach than the first half.

With a little under two minutes left in the game and the Jets on what will most likely be their last possession, they are down by three. Tanner takes a hard sack in the backfield making it now fourth and longer than anyone would like. When everyone gets into formation I notice Tanner's limping to the line.

"What's going on?" I ask Andrew worried that maybe he was seriously hurt on that last play.

"I'm not sure. It was a hard hit but not that hard," he answers never taking his eyes off the field as the ball is snapped.

Tanner drops back into the backfield faster than anyone was expecting after he was just seemingly hurt. He takes a second to read the field before he finds an open receiver. It feels like the ball hangs in the air for a lifetime before it hits Sparks' hands. As soon as the defense realizes where the pass is going, they all head toward Sparks, who doesn't have a significant lead on them. One of the guys from the Cardinals gets his hands on him right before the goal line and they fall onto the goal line in a mess of bodies.

Silence.

The stadium is uncharacteristically quiet and the refs pull guy after guy off of the pile-up in the end zone as they try to determine if it was, in fact, a game-changing touchdown. The ref throws his hand up signaling touchdown and the crowd erupts in riotous cheers. The extra point is good and now all they have to do is hold Arizona for thirty-two seconds.

I watch Tanner as he paces the sidelines. He hates when the fate of the game isn't in his hands. He hates having to watch from the sidelines in situations like this, but there isn't anything he can do about it. Tanner is now crouched down as there's ten seconds left on the clock and its fourth and one. Arizona's quarterback throws the ball, but it never hits the receiver as our corner, Kelvin, slaps the ball down. Tanner jumps up and the entire sideline breaks out into celebration as Tanner is hoisted up on his team's shoulders!

Tanner just won the fucking super bowl!

Oh, my god! I watch as the fans pour onto the field, like ants at a picnic.

All of my anxiety is replaced with pride. I'm so damn proud of him. I've been waiting for the dark clouds of the past to roll in, but there is no room for them with all the love and respect currently consuming me.

We have our own celebration in the suite as we watch everything unfold down on the field. It's a freaking jungle down there and I see why Tanner didn't want me down there dealing with all of that. We watch the presentation for both the Lombardi trophy and the MVP trophy, which goes to Tanner.

As all the partying starts to break down, Quinn pulls me aside, "I know this is a huge night for you guys and all, but I'm going to head out before you guys meet up with Tanner. I'm sure Alex won't be too far behind and I just can't deal with all that right now."

"You sure you don't want to stay?" I ask hoping she'll reconsider. She's my best friend and I selfishly want to celebrate all the good things in my life with her.

"Yeah, I'm more than sure. Tell Superstar I said job well done," she smiles sadly before breaking away from the group and heading in the opposite direction.

I truly wish those two would work through whatever their shit is, but I don't have time to dwell on their disaster. I have a hubby to find and celebrate with.

Chapter Nine

ASHLEY

"**YOU ALMOST READY** to go, baby?" Tanner yells from the bedroom. He's been not so patiently waiting for me to put the 'finishing touches' on my ensemble for the last twenty minutes.

"Yes, almost," I tell him for the second time since I escaped into the bathroom. I should have taken Quinn up on her offer to set me up with the 'hair and makeup stylist for the stars'. I'm not a star and laughed at Quinn's dumb suggestion. Not thinking it's so dumb now, though.

I feel like the pregnancy is having a negative effect on every part of my body. My boobs are huge and jiggly, making me feel top heavy. I've always had a very nice "C" cup, but now I'm a "DD". My ass should have its own zip code at this point and my skin looks lackluster. Basically, I'm a huge not-so-hot mess these days and I still have five months to go.

Dress shopping for this event, a fundraiser for a new group home The Mathis Foundation is trying to break ground on, was nothing short of a fucking nightmare. No matter what I put on, I felt like I was trying to squeeze ten pounds of shit into a five-pound bag. I wanted something flowy and cute to hide my ever changing body and Quinn insisted on something sexier.

"You know, not everyone is a size two, blonde haired, blue eyed bombshell with perfect tits and a fantastic ass, Quinn," I told her when she brought a bunch of dresses to the dressing room of Bergdorf's when we were shopping last week.

"Stop with your pity party. You look beautiful. I'm not your pussy-whipped husband so don't fish for compliments from me." She practically threw the dresses at me when she finished with her little rant. She's been more of a bitch than usual lately.

"I'm not fishing for compliments, you mean twat. I just can't squeeze my now larger ass into these little excuses for dresses you want me to wear." I could be a bitch too! These hormones are making me more irritable than I remember being with Daniel.

"Try them on and shut the hell up. I'm not above hitting a pregnant chick."

Needless to say, I'm squeezed into a tighter than I'd like, one-shouldered, blue Gucci dress that hugs more curves than I'd like it too.

Giving up on fussing with my hair and make-up any longer, I apply my lipstick, which is a shade of red that goes perfectly with my dress and call it a day. I'm a writer, not a magician. This is as good as it's going to get.

I stroll into our bedroom with much less enthusiasm for this evening than I had when I first found out about it. I start my search for where I left my new strappy black Prada heels. I could have sworn I left them on the bench at the end of our bed, but who the hell knows what I did with them. My brain is fried. I feel like I should be committed. I'm all over the place lately.

I'm on my hands and knees looking for them under the bed when Tanner emerges from our closet, chuckling. "Not that I'm complaining about the lovely view, but what the hell are you doing?"

"Nobody would enjoy this view," I snap at him. "I'm looking for my damn shoes." Sighing as I realize they aren't under my bed, I make my way ungracefully to my feet and turn my attention to my smug ass husband who looks downright delectable in his three-piece, black Armani suit.

"You mean these shoes?" he says. My shoes indeed hanging off his long index finger. "And yes, I was enjoying the view. Undoubtedly."

"Yes, those shoes," I say walking over to snatch them from his hand but ignore his comment about my ass. He's obligated to say I look good. Well, he is if he wants to live in a tension free home and get laid.

"What's got you all riled up, Ash?" he asks sitting down next to me as I put on my shoes.

"Nothing."

"Nothing never means nothing in woman talk. Even I know that," he says with a smirk on his face that makes me just want to junk punch him. I know it's not his fault he looks so fucking good and I don't, but I'm not about to get into it with him since I know he's going to tell me I look good. He doesn't have a choice but to say that.

"I'm just moody, that's all," I tell him I as buckle the last strap on my shoes. "I'm ready."

"Okay, beautiful. Let's get moving then," he says with his huge mega-watt smile as he extends his hand to help me up from the bed. "But don't think for a second that I believe you're just moody."

THIS EVENT IS nothing short of spectacular, as is every event The Mathis Foundation holds. You would think going with a theme that included red a few days before Valentine's Day would be tacky, but they pulled it off beautifully. Everything is a glittery silver color with red accents including roses. I wonder if any of the florists in the city will have any roses left on Valentine's Day. Guess all the poor schmucks who waited until the last minute are screwed. Karma got their asses this Valentine's Day.

We're barely through the main doors when Tanner is practically bum rushed by Maria, the event coordinator for this evening.

"Tanner, I'm so glad you're here," she rushes out practically frantic. I can't imagine how stressful her job is. "Hello, Ashley. So good to see you again," she says to me before returning her attention to Tanner.

"Okay, so a few of the big guys we need to really schmooze are already here. Wallace and Stockham are floating around here somewhere and I've been instructed to tell you that you should start with them first. Both have expressed interest in donating some big bucks. So pose, take pictures and kiss their asses. We've seated all the top possible investors at the table adjacent to yours so that they can be talked to all night long."

I tune her out as she rambles on about how the board wants Tanner to woo them. Wallace has one foot in the grave and has more money than he knows what to do with. He's some former investment broker and back in his day everything he touched turned to gold. Stockham is a big real estate investor. Like huge. He's another that has the golden touch but only with real estate and land development. That's where his luck ends. He also likes women and is apparently looking for wife number five. Tanner told me a little about these important players tonight on the way over. I'm thankful he didn't tell me any earlier because I would've forgotten everything I was supposed to remember in order to be the good wife and make conversation with these pompous asses.

"Okay, well if you need me just text me," Maria says bringing me back to the conversation happening around me. "Right now I need to settle a pissing match between the head chef and the pastry chef in the kitchen. Grown men fighting in the middle of a huge event. Because my job isn't crazy enough." Then she's gone in a blur of purple as her dress flurries all around her in her haste to get to the next problem that needs to be concurred.

"She's small, but hell if I want to be on her bad side," Tanner laughs as he watches her scurry out of the ballroom.

As we weave our way through the crowd, I spot someone that fits the description Tanner gave me of Mr. Stockham. Tall, blonde with a dorky haircut that screams mid-life crisis. I feel the aura he gives off from here. Entitlement. He says something and then laughs like it was the funniest thing that has ever been said. The group around him breaks out in forced laughter that screams 'let me kiss your ass'. He has a date draped over him like a rash. I can't see her face since she's facing him with her back turned to us, but I can see the obnoxiously bright, albeit, beautiful red gown. Her entire back is on display. I can't help the little bit of jealousy that seeps in while I take in her amazing figure.

"Is that Stockham?" I ask, pointing him out to Tanner with a nod of my head.

"Yeah," he confirms. "Let's go get him out of the way first." With a hand at the small of my back, he guides me toward the group where he is. As we take our first steps toward them, his date turns revealing her identity to us.

"You've got to be fucking kidding me," Tanner growls. Not his sexy growl that usually has my panties melt instantly but his annoyed one.

I freeze, momentarily stunned. You've got to be kidding me is right! She's the last person I want to see on a good day, let alone a bad day.

"We don't have a choice," I point out. "Let's just get this shit over with."

"I'm sorry you're going to have to deal with her," Tanner says remorsefully.

"It's not your fault," I tell him sincerely. It's not. I wish I didn't have to face her since I'd like nothing more than to break her face, but it is what it is. I've gotten the best of her the last time we had to be in the same company so let's hope the pattern will continue.

"Mr. Stockham," Tanner says managing to smile as he greets this man.

"Mr. Garrison, such a pleasure to meet you," Stockham smiles larger than life as he offers his hand for Tanner to shake.

"Likewise," Tanner says. "This is my beautiful wife, Ashley," he says with the smile he reserves just for me. No one other than me would know that Tanner is trying to ease my nerves in this situation.

"Pleasure," Stockham responds wrapping his arm around his date as he brings her forth to introduce us as if that's needed. Obviously, Stockham has no knowledge that we all unfortunately already know each other.

"This is my lovely girlfriend, Melissa Finnegan," he says as his introduction to this vile creation standing next him. The word lovely should never be used when referring to Melissa. Compared to this bitch, herpes is lovely.

"Melissa," Tanner says with complete distaste in his voice. Anyone looking close enough at him while he uttered her name would have noticed the tick in his jaw.

"Tanner. Ashley. So wonderful seeing you again." The fakeness in her voice is enough to make me vomit on her ridiculously high heels.

Neither Tanner nor I respond to her greeting and her oblivious date doesn't pick up on the tension so thick you could cut it with a knife. "I didn't realize you knew each other," he says. With all the money this asshole has, you think he'd buy a fucking clue.

"Jonathan, do you think you could get us another round of drinks before you boys start talking shop?" Melissa says, her fake sugary voice grates further on my nerves with each word that leaves her mouth.

“Of course, my dear,” he says like the total tool he is and goes off to do Melissa’s bidding.

“Ashley, you’re looking larger these days,” the bitch says not wasting a beat to insult me.

“That would be because I’m pregnant, you twat,” I grit out trying my best not to let this evil woman get to me. But as always, she knows right where to hit for the best impact.

“Really?” she says leaning around to look at something behind me. “I didn’t know that women were carrying babies in their asses these days. You shouldn’t try to pass off bad ass implants as being pregnant.” I don’t know why the nerve of this woman continues to amaze me. I mean she sent me a sympathy card telling me my little problem had a way of working itself out. I think it’s her uncanny ability to always find my weak spot and push it as hard as she can. I already feel uncomfortable in my own new skin, I don’t need this woman pointing out my new flaws

“Careful, Melissa. Green has never been a good color on you and you wouldn’t want your latest victim to see you for who you really are so soon, would you?” Tanner says coming to my defense.

“I don’t think it matters either way, baby,” I say forcing a fake smile at him. ”She’d be his fifth wife. I’m sure he’s no stranger to the gold digger game. She’d have to sign a prenup. So while she has to keep fucking him, and fucking him well, for his money, I get you, which is what this bitch always wanted anyway.” I really channeled my inner Quinn there. If she were here, she’d be so proud.

“Unless you keep getting bigger. A whining kid and fat wife have never been Tanner’s style. He’ll be crawling back to the ‘me’s of the world faster than you can turn your head with its extra chins.” I want nothing more than to snap back with some extra brilliant comeback to put her in her place, but I can’t. She has just put a voice to my biggest insecurity right now. Over the last month, my body has changed so much that I’m completely self-conscience when I haven’t been that way with my body since puberty.

“Listen here, you stupid cunt, I wouldn’t come back to you, or anyone like you, if you were the last piece of pussy on the planet. Not even if you told me I had to use or lose it. I’d rather lose it than stick my dick anywhere within a fifty-foot radius of you.” Tanner’s voice is low and menacing, causing her to literally laugh at us. She’s not dumb. She knows she just hit me with an uppercut.

Nobody has a chance to say anything more before Stockham comes back with drinks and smiles again, completely unaware of the rigidity around him. “I have to say I’m pretty excited to be a part of this new project. I think I’ve got the perfect location for it off of 440 on Staten Island between Mariner’s Harbor and Port Richmond. A few buildings were just leveled and I’m positive I can get a great deal on the land. I’d be more than happy to gift it to the foundation for the building.”

“That sounds wonderful. I’m sure the board will be extremely happy with your donation, it’s very generous of you. The community in that area is in desperate need of a community center. We’ll really be able to make a difference.” I know Tanner is genuinely pleased this man is offering such great things for the kids but even so, with that wretched woman on his arm it’s almost hard to be grateful for anything from him.

Chapter Ten

TANNER

I CAN'T GET away from this man quick enough. Continuing to be in the presence of Melissa after all the bullshit she just spewed at Ashley is making me close to losing my shit. The insecurity is rolling off Ashley in waves so strong, I feel she may drown in them.

"I'll propose the location to them first thing Monday morning and get their thoughts before striking up any deals for the lots," Stockham adds before finishing the drink he just came back with. I'd need copious amounts of alcohol to deal with the dreaded bitch on his arm too.

"Fantastic. Please enjoy the rest of your evening," I say offering my hand and hoping to escape before Melissa opens that awful mouth of hers again.

I grab Ashley's hand and entwine my fingers with hers before dragging her back toward the front of the room. I know there's a small little room they use for wedding parties to wait out cocktail hour near the entrance.

"Where are we going?" she asks confused as I drag her behind me without a word. I don't even acknowledge the people speaking to me with more than a nod and a hello. I have a problem to solve.

I know that she's been unhappy with the way her body has been changing over the last few months and I hate that it bothers her. I know that's what had her all up in arms before we left tonight but I was hoping that she would talk to me about it. But after Melissa's direct hit to Ashley's insecurities, I know I don't have time to let her hurt fester.

I pull her into the room, which isn't being used tonight, and lock the door behind me.

"Tanner, what the hell are you doing? You have a room of people you're supposed to be working." Ashley says. There's frustration and pain mixed in her voice.

"I have a wife who needs me more at the moment," I tell her, pulling on her hand to bring her closer to me.

"What are you talking about?" she says now annoyed.

"I know what that evil bitch said hurt you," I say wrapping my hand around the nape of her neck, pulling her close to me so I can rest my forehead on hers.

"It is what it is. This is not the time or place to talk about it," she says trying to pull away from me.

"Yes, it is. I know why you were so grouchy before we left also. I'm not letting you walk around here all night questioning what she said. There's no merit to it, baby."

"It's not like it isn't true, I just hate that she had to be the one to say it." Her voice is so small it breaks my heart. I've never seen this side of Ashley. Yes, I've seen her vulnerable but never in this capacity. I need to fix it and now.

"It's not true. Not one word of what she said. You're beautiful today. Just like you were yesterday, just like you will be tomorrow and the day after that. I love the way you look. I always have and I always will. What don't you get about that? You're the only one unhappy with this," I tell her as I run my hands all over her body, touching any place I can get my hands on. Simply being in the same space as Ashley turns me on. My hands on her body, the body growing our child is enough to make my dick hard enough to pound nails.

"You're my husband, you have to say that. Just because you say it doesn't make it true." *Is she kidding me?* I guess I haven't been doing enough lately to make her feel sexy. Christ, there's nothing sexier than Ashley, ever. A little baby weight or not. And by a little, I mean a little. To me, she barely looks pregnant. But what the fuck do I know when it comes to a woman's feeling about her body while with child.

Grabbing her hand, I place it on my dick which is testing the durability of the zipper of my pants. "Does anything about this rock hard cock feel like a lie? There isn't one thing about you that doesn't make me want to rip your clothes off and fuck you until you can't walk."

I hear her gasp, but I'm not done yet. I circle her, stopping behind her and unzip the zipper down the back of her dress and slip the single strap down her shoulder, kissing each inch of skin I expose. When I get the dress down enough to free both of her beautiful tits, I cup them gently in my hands, kneading slowly before rolling her rosy tips between my thumbs and forefinger. I know how sensitive they've become and I love nothing more than watching Ashley fall apart just from my fingers playing with her perfectly pebbled nipples.

"I'm like a kid in a candy store with all these new little treasures your body now has to offer. You know I love nothing more than finding new ways to set you off. These right here were perfect before, they're perfect now, and they'll be perfect when this is all over, regardless of any changes. These babies are attached to you which makes them flawless regardless of anything else," I explain as I come around to her front again. I lower my head and pull one of those pretty peeks into my mouth using my teeth, causing the throatiest moan I've ever heard leave her mouth. Fuck me if that doesn't make me practically come in my pants.

"You keep moaning like that and my three thousand dollar suit pants are going to have a rather large cum stain on them." She moans louder. I'm about to blow my load in my pants like a teenager about to get his first taste of pussy. And my wife is doubting her hotness.

Pulling her dress down until it pools around her feet, I squat down and place a few kisses on her belly. "This. I love this more than I can ever express. In here you hold the most precious thing in my life other than you. That on its own is a beautiful thing."

"Please, Tanner. Now is not the time for slow. Someone is probably looking for you right now," she says as if I give two shits about anything other than making my wife happy at the moment.

"There's only one person who I care about right now." I clarify for her as I stand and circle back around her to get a full view of her now exposed ass. Grabbing one glorious globe in each hand, I squeeze hard enough to make Ashley squeal. "And this, goddamn, is this one marvelous ass! Every time you bend over, giving me the greatest view in the world, all I can think about is squeezing them around my cock and sliding through your ass cheeks until you make me come all over them."

And that's the God's honest truth. I've pictured fucking just her ass cheeks over and over again. We will definitely be doing that soon. Maybe even when I get her home tonight, since now might not be the time for me to 'Monica Lewinski' all over her dress.

Leaning her head back against my shoulder she snorts, "Even after all these years, I'm still shocked at the dirty things that leave your mouth."

Instead of responding to her statement with my mouth, even though I'm extremely pleased that I can continue to keep shocking her, I respond with my fingers delving into her pussy.

"And this. This is my personal paradise. Your pussy is magic. Always has been. Its smell, its taste, the way it strangles the life out of my cock when you come. I love it. I'm the luckiest asshole in the world because I get to enjoy this pussy and everything that comes with it, every single day. You're perfect, baby. Every single part of you. If you can't believe it coming from my mouth, then I'll make you believe it with my dick."

"Fuck," she whimpers. I can feel the surge of wetness my words have caused on my fingers. I want to take my hands and beat on my chest knowing I can get my girl dripping with just my words.

I grab her leg and prop it up on the small end table by the side of the couch before dropping back to my knees. Burying my face in her ass, I waste no time and begin to lap at the juice pooling in my favorite place on Earth. I hold Ash in place when her legs start to wobble but never stop my ministration on her core. The walls of her pussy start to quake and I make fast work of my belt and zipper before standing.

"Bend over the couch, baby. I want to watch that fabulous ass jiggle as I prove to you with my cock just how sexy you are." That is the only warning my self-doubting wife gets before I drive my point home. My balls slap her clit so hard she comes instantly screaming my name.

"Oh, God! Oh, my God, Tanner! Fuck! Ahh," she chants over and over. I'm supposed to be building her confidence with this, but fuck if she isn't making me feel like the master of her universe.

"That's right, baby! Do you still feel unattractive with my cock buried inside you? Because let me tell you, you feel like the best damn thing ever. I don't think I can last much longer. That's how fucking hot you are."

"Shit! Oh, my god, I'm going to come again," she says as she starts to move her hips faster, meeting me thrust for thrust. These are some of the moments I live for. The moments when Ashley is so far gone in pleasure, she loses all composure. Moments when she fucks herself with my cock.

"Come now, baby. I'm coming with you." And we do. We come together in a blur of moans and pure ecstasy. I've lost all ability to move so I just remain seated inside Ashley and enjoy the little tremors of her pussy. My head resting on Ashley's back, I listen to the sounds of her erratic breathing and hope to hell that I've proved to her she's the sexiest woman in the world to me, a few extra pounds or not!

"Please don't ever doubt your beauty. Nothing in the world could ever change the way I see you. Ever." I whisper into her ear before removing myself from her body. I try to ignore the sudden loss of her warmth by telling myself I'll be buried right back in there as soon as we walk through the front door tonight.

"If that's what I get when I'm feeling insecure, it's not much of a reason to feel good about myself," she chuckles.

"You'll always get that, because one look at you, anytime, anywhere, has me holding on to my self-control by the skin of my teeth," I tell her before molding my mouth to hers and giving her a kiss she won't soon forget.

Chapter Eleven

TANNER

I KNEW I needed to do something special for Ashley after I saw how down she was feeling about herself at the fundraiser. Thankfully, this is where having two sisters comes in. When I told Veronica and Beth about my plans, they told me there's apparently this thing called a babymoon. It's basically like a honeymoon but only a vacation before the baby arrives. I laughed while they were explaining this and asked if people really did this shit or they were just messing with me. I googled it when I didn't believe them and found out not only was is true, but there were places that actually specialized in this shit.

I didn't want to take her somewhere too public. Having just won the Super Bowl, I didn't want unwanted attention. Taking a little bit of everything from all these places' websites to make my own private getaway for the two of us, I decided to rent a villa on a private island in the Bahamas.

It didn't dawn on me to check with her doctor until after I made all the reservations. When I called his office I prayed like hell he was going to tell me it was okay. I was good as long as I took her before the third trimester. I had no idea what the hell the third trimester was so again this was when having sisters was beneficial. Everything was okay since I wanted to take her right away. I'm glad I decided that getting out of here while it's cold was the best plan. I thought about taking her to some of the lake towns here in the US but the Poconos and Lake Tahoe are still cold at the beginning of March. I wanted to be somewhere warm and secluded. Besides, we have a house in Lake Tahoe and I can take her there anytime I want.

I've kept the whole thing a secret. I worked everything out for work with Dom, her boss, and had Quinn buy her a whole new wardrobe for the trip. I had to remind Quinn not to pick all sexy things since I know that would make Ash feel even worse about herself. Quinn can be fucking nuts sometimes.

Standing at the end of our bed, I look at my beautiful wife trying to figure out the best way to break this to her. I know that she's going to have a million excuses as to why this is a bad idea but she's not getting a say in this. I'm actually more than excited to get away with her, just us, for a while.

I pull the comforter and sheets from the bed, exposing her gorgeous sleeping form. I love that she only sleeps in panties. I love those lacy little short things, especially when they are the only thing she's wearing. I start kissing her calf and work my way up. By the time I get to her belly, she's started stirring. "Mmm," she moans out. She's going to be disappointed when she realizes I'm not waking her for sex. Too bad, we have almost a whole week for that. She hasn't opened her eyes by the time I reach her neck, but her moaning and squirming have picked up. When I get to the little spot behind her ear that always drives her mad I whisper, "Time to wake up, sleeping beauty."

"I don't need to be awake for you to have your wicked way with me," she grumbles.

"But I'm not having my wicked way with you right now and you need to be awake for what I have planned," I say before smacking her ass and jumping off the bed.

"What the hell? You wake me up with the promise of an orgasm and then leave me hanging? That's fucked up." Have I mentioned that Ashley is not a morning person while pregnant?

"Okay. Then I'll go on this romantic vacation by myself and you can stay here complaining about your lack of orgasms. As if you didn't have two spectacular ones last night. You're getting really greedy lately," I yell as I disappear into the closet.

"Vacation? What vacation? I can't go on vacation and you know it," she protests, as predicted.

"Yes, you can. Now, get your fine ass out of bed and get ready. The plane leaves in two hours." I wait patiently for the yelling.

"Two hours? What the hell, Tanner? I can't pack and clear things with work and the doctor and be ready in an hour." I should get an award for the ability to predict my wife's behavior.

"Yes, you can. Now get up and get ready." Three… Two….One…

"No, I can't! You can't just spring a surprise vacation on me. I don't even know if I can fly at this point. I didn't clear this with work and I don't even know where we're going or what to pack! You didn't think this through at all, did you?" she yells angrily from the bedroom where I can hear her stomping around. Her bratty ways will not ruin my good mood. I'll haul her ass over my shoulder if I have too.

Walking out of the closet with her already packed suitcase in hand, I gently inform her, "I have thought this through. Every single detail. Your suitcase is already packed. I've already cleared this trip with Dom and Dr. Marcus. Apparently, this babymoon thing is very popular and Dom said you can use this as a piece for work if you want. Now, all you have to do is stop being a whiny brat and get your hot ass in the shower. Put on something light, we're going somewhere warm."

"You planned a babymoon?" she says, her voice cracking. "And you took care of everything?" Okay, the tears I didn't see coming.

Dropping the suitcase on the bed, I grab her and pull her into my arms. "Yes, but why are you crying?"

"Because I read about these trips and I wanted one but didn't want to ask. And now you've planned one and I yelled at you like a bitchy, ungrateful wife. I'm sorry." Shit! These hormones are crazy! I can't keep up.

"Baby, if you wanted one you should have asked. You know I'll give you anything you want. You're not an ungrateful bitch. Now, go shower so we can make our flight." I try to placate her, but I'm out of my depth here.

It seems to have worked because she heads for the shower, so I make sure I have everything ready to load into the car when it arrives.

IT ISN'T UNTIL after we've taken off I give into Ashley's incessant demands to know where we're going. I wanted to try and keep it a secret, but with the way her emotions are all over the place today, I decided to just tell her instead of running the risk of pissing her off.

"The Bahamas," I admit after the fifth time she's asked in ten minutes.

"Ohh, Atlantis?" she questions with a giddy smile on her face. Shit if Atlantis would've made her happy, I could have saved a shit ton of money on this trip.

"No, baby, not Atlantis. A small private island where I rented a villa. There're only two other villas on the island and I reserved those for the staff I've hired. It's just going to be me and you." I'm more than stoked to have an entire five days of Ashley all to myself. No one pulling me in this direction or that direction. Just peace and quiet.

"You've rented an entire island for just us?" she asks as if I just told her I chartered a plane to Jupiter.

"Yes. No one to bother us. Just you and me," I say wiggling my eyebrows at her suggestively.

"Wow! Won't we get bored all by ourselves after the first day?" She has no faith in me at all.

I smile as I answer her, "No, baby, I've planned you the best babymoon ever known to woman."

This piques her interest even more since she bolts upright in her chair and smiles broadly at me. "What do you have planned?"

"I'm not telling you. Something about this trip has to be a surprise."

Chapter Twelve

ASHLEY

TANNER WASN'T KIDDING when he said he planned the babymoon of all babymoons. It was five days of pure pampering. All set up by my wonderful husband. We did nothing but relax on the first two days. It was a very weird experience to be waited on hand and foot by people. Something I'm definitely not used to. We live very comfortably, but we've never had more than a housekeeper. Yes, she does the cooking, the cleaning, and the grocery shopping but she doesn't wait on us. I don't think it's something I could ever really get used to. Tanner told me to just enjoy it because soon I won't have any downtime so I should sit around and do nothing. Even a vacation would be work soon. So I sat back and enjoyed.

The place was beautiful. It was the whole tropical experience. The villa was large and open. The sun shone in from every angle. The windows were covered with just sheer white curtains that blew with the breeze like a scene out of a movie. It was so close to the water, it was like having one of those sound machines near your bed at night.

The weather was perfect and the water was gorgeous. Our third day, we went snorkeling and Tanner chartered a catamaran to take us around the islands. The fourth day was a day of pampering including massages, facials, a mani-pedi for me and a quiet dinner on the deck of the villa, which included dessert of my husband. The baby decided it was very impressed with all of daddy's surprises for mommy because that night while in bed, the baby decided to finally allow Tanner to feel his or her presence.

"Oh my god," I gasped, frightening Tanner.

"What? What's wrong?" he asked jackknifing up in bed.

"The baby," I told him not giving any more of an explanation because I was still so astonished by the power of this little one.

"What? What about the baby?" he pressed looking completely terrified.

"It's kicking. Hard." I explained, grabbing his hand and placing it over my belly.

The look that overtook Tanner's face when he felt our child for the first time is a look I don't think I'll ever forget.

"Wow," he uttered astonished before leaning his head down to my belly to speak to the baby. "Hi, little one. It's Daddy. We feel you in there. Are you enjoying all the relaxing Mommy is doing? You be good in there. I love you."

We both had tears in our eyes as he spoke.

Tanner wrapped himself around me as we spent the rest of the night waiting for more kicks from our precious little one before falling into a very blissful sleep.

It was almost impossible to top that day, but Tanner went all out for the last day. He planned a maternity photo shoot. Never did I expect that. He was worried I would be upset because most people did this later in their pregnancies. When he explained that we couldn't pass up the beautiful scenery, I knew he was right. The photos came out stunning and I can't wait to hang them in the nursery. I spent the entire flight home discussing where they'd look best with Tanner until he pointed out that we'd need to really see the finished product in person. I don't know how, I'm sure Tanner must have paid extra, but the photos arrived by courier three days after we returned. They were more beautiful than I could have imagined. I actually cried when I pulled them from their packaging. Tanner thought I was upset because I didn't like them. When I told him I was crying because I love them he muttered something about crazy hormones and shook his head.

I'VE BEEN THINKING non-stop about the nursery since we arrived home from the Bahamas. The biggest part of the nursery is the theme. Tanner and I had already discussed finding out the sex of the baby, but now that the time to know has finally arrived I'm having second thoughts.

"I know we already discussed this, but now I'm not so sure I want to wait to find out," I inform him as we make our way to the doctor's office. Today is the day the doctor is doing my big ultrasound. I'm twenty-two weeks along and we can find out the sex of the baby if we want. I could've found out weeks ago, but we were set on keeping it a surprise.

"Why the change of heart?" he asks, with a surprised expression on his face. I've told him before that after losing Daniel it doesn't matter to me one way or the other what we're having as long as he or she is healthy. Tanner agreed and thus we decided to go the surprise route.

"I want to have the perfect nursery. I want to hang those beautiful photos on the wall and I don't really think yellow or green is going to cut it for me."

"Green is a great color," Tanner says obviously referring to his team color.

I huff. "Yeah, green is great. For a boy. I don't want my daughter in a green room."

"Okay, then go with yellow," he says.

"I've read online that yellow can be overly stimulating for the baby," I say even though people have been doing yellow rooms for years, I'm just not feeling the yellow.

"Well, we could always wait and have the nursery done after the baby comes," he offers as if that's the perfect solution.

"No. Part of the whole mother-to-be thing is planning out the nursery. I don't want to do it after the baby is here and I'm trying to adjust to being a new mom. And you won't even be around all that much. You'll be at training camp and I'll be stuck at home with creepy carpenters by myself." He just doesn't seem to understand that I need to have everything perfect, including this. I need to have all this planned out ahead of time. Especially if I'll be spending most days home alone with the baby.

Not that I'm complaining about getting to spend all day with my baby. I'd just prefer to do it in a quiet house with no construction and a nursery planned specifically to fit my child and not for two possibilities.

"We can find out if that's what you really want. I just want to make sure that you're sure about this. Once we find out, we can't un-know."

We debate this back and forth right up until Lacey comes to the door and calls me into my appointment.

Fifteen minutes later, I'm up on the table, belly exposed, waiting to hear the beautiful sound of my little's heartbeat.

"Are we finding out the sex today?" Dr. Marcus asks as he rolls the wand all over my belly taking his measurements of the baby.

I lock eyes with Tanner, pleading for him to see my points on this. He smiles at me before answering the doctor, "Yes."

I don't take my eyes from his until the doctor says, "Well this right here," he points to the screen, "would be where the penis would be if you were having a son but you're not. Congratulations, it's a girl."

A girl.

Wow, I didn't care one way or the other but we're having a daughter. I look at Tanner just in time to see him wipe away a tear that rolled down his face. "You're right, a green room definitely wouldn't have been good enough for my little princess."

Chapter Thirteen

ASHLEY

THE SADNESS I usually feel when I come here doesn't feel as heavy today. But there is something else I'm feeling. I can't quite put my finger on it, but it's a different kind of sadness. Sadness for the loss of the big brother my little girl would've had instead of sadness for what I've lost.

It's a beautiful spring day today, which I'm pretty sure is helping keep the sorrow at bay. It's fairly warm for the first week of April. The birds are chirping, the flowers are starting to bloom and the leaves on the trees are beginning to grow back. Everything looks bright and healthy. It's hard to feel depressed on a day like this. I feel as though this a reminder that there's still good in the world, and I should be happy for all the good I still have in my life, even if Daniel couldn't physically be a part of that world.

I kneel and place the multicolored Gerber daisies in the built-in vase at the bottom of Daniel's headstone. I brush away the stray grass and leaves stuck to the bottom of it, which must be from the last time they trimmed the grounds.

"Hi sweetheart," I say staring at that single date representing Daniel's life. "I'm sorry Mommy hasn't been here in a little while. It's still kind of hard to think about leaving you here. But I wanted to come in person today to tell you about your baby sister."

I pull the extra sonogram picture I brought from my pocket and place it next the flowers.

"She's beautiful! Just like you." I wipe a stray tear from my cheek. I've gotten a lot better when coming here. It still hurts but not as though someone is ripping my heart out through my chest.

"I wish you could be here for her as she grows up. I didn't have a big brother, but I hear it's really a great thing for a girl to have. I know you would've been the best. You'll still be the best just in a different way. I'm really happy she will have you looking out for her." I let a few stray tears roll down my cheeks as I turn my face up to the sun and let it warm me. I choose to believe the warmth is Daniel's way of lifting me up. A warm hug from Heaven.

"I'm scared. I couldn't protect you, what if I can't protect her either?" I say finally finding the strength to voice my biggest fear out loud.

"I will protect you both," Tanner says from behind me, startling the shit out of me.

"What are you doing here?" I ask, shocked he knew I'd be here.

"I knew something was bothering you and you weren't talking to me about it. I figured it had something to do with your fears resurfacing. So when you left earlier just telling me you were going out, I guessed you'd be coming here. I don't know why really, just a feeling I had. Guess my hunch was right," he says closing the distance between us. When he finally reaches me, Tanner drops to the ground behind me and pulls me between his legs, crushing my body to his. "Why didn't you think you could talk to me about this, baby?"

"It's not that I didn't think I couldn't talk to you about it. It's just I feel like a failure already and what if I fail again? What if I can't protect her, just like I couldn't protect Daniel? Look at how one little scare rattled my cage. I won't survive another loss, Tanner. I won't."

"Ashley, you didn't fail, sweetheart. You were hit by a drunk driver. You had no control over the situation. I don't know many people who could have protected their child any better than you did in the situation you were in," he says squeezing his arms tighter around me and kissing the top of my head.

"Does it really matter what I did, if at the end of the day I didn't manage to save our child? Maybe I don't have what it takes to be a good mother." I whisper my biggest fear aloud. What if I'm just not cut out to be a mother? Lord knows mine wasn't. Maybe it's genetic.

"We've been over this before, baby. Daniel is where he was meant to be. We may never understand it but for some reason, he was meant to watch us from above. And now he will watch over her too," he says cupping his hands around my belly, cradling not only our daughter but me. The strength and conviction in his words give me the power I need to feel as though everything just might be okay this time around. "You will be a fantastic mother. You should never doubt that. I don't doubt you. I never have. There isn't any other person in the world I would rather have as the mother of my children."

"I'm still scared." Like he said earlier, some things are just out of our control and you can't make things turn out perfectly on sheer determination alone.

"I know you are, but I want you to always know that no matter what, I will protect the both of you and any future children we have. Until my dying breath. I've got you, baby. Never doubt that." I know how sincere he is in his promise, but nothing other than time will erase this fear.

Tanner and I sit in a peaceful silence as we visit with our son. There isn't much else to say right now. Now Tanner knows my deepest fears and I have no doubt he will reassure me every step of the way.

“What else is bothering you, baby?” he asks using his super power of deduction to figure out there’s something else weighing on me.

“I don’t want to have another C-section,” I sigh thinking back to the conversation we had with Dr. Marcus about this at our doctor’s appointment earlier this week. “I want to bring our daughter into the world myself, not have the doctors remove her for me.”

Tanner kisses the top of my head before responding. “He didn’t say you couldn’t, he just wanted to discuss the risks with you.”

“He also didn’t say I could.” I realistically know the doctor can’t know how things will go, but I wish he could tell me that everything will go just fine. I wish he’d tell me everything will turn out how I want it to this time around.

“He said you’re a candidate for regular birth after a C-section. There isn’t anything you can do one way or another to make sure it happens. He said he’ll allow for you to try. If it doesn’t work then you have the C-section. Stop stressing about the things you can’t control,” he says kissing my temple while rubbing my belly.

“I know I can’t control it, but it doesn’t change my feelings about it. It’s just something else about becoming a mother I’ll fail at,” I sigh. He just doesn’t understand the need I feel to bring this baby in on my own. I didn’t have a choice with Daniel and I don’t want to watch my child brought into the world while I’m strapped to a table, unable to hold her for lord knows how long.

“Having another C-Section won’t make you a failure Ashley. Women have them every single day. Does that make them failures as mothers?” he asks.

“No, that’s not what I’m saying. It would just make me feel like I failed again.” He doesn’t get where I’m coming from and I can’t really explain it.

“No matter how this baby enters the world, you’ll never be a failure as a mother. This baby isn’t even here yet and you’re already a fantastic mother. Will we stumble at this thing from time to time? Of course, we will. Our parents did. Their parents did. There’s no manual for this, sweetheart. Everyone stumbles. There is no such thing as the perfect parent. If that's what you're striving for, you're only setting yourself up for disappointment. And nothing about this journey should be a disappointment." His words are a balm to my soul. He's right. I can't be perfect all the time, especially when it comes to this. I just have to give my all and hope it's enough.

"You always seem to know just the right words to say to make me feel better," I tell him turning my head to smile up at him.

"And I always will, as long as you talk to me. I don't like that you felt the need to carry this burden around by yourself. I'm always here for you, Ashley, no matter what the problem is," he says bringing his lips down to meet mine. And just like that, at this moment, with my husband and our children, I feel content.

Chapter Fourteen

ASHLEY

"**WHAT THE HELL** do you mean you don't want a baby shower?" Quinn scoffs finishing off the rest of her sandwich. She's here for our weekly girl time. We've gotten together once a week since I moved in with Tanner.

"I mean I don't want a shower. I don't want to have a party to celebrate something that hasn't happened yet." I explain. I don't expect her to understand. A lot of people who haven't been through what I have wouldn't understand.

"Baby showers are a rite of passage. It's practically a requirement for pregnant women," she says her hands flying frantically as she argues her point.

"I don't want one. It's bad luck. I don't want a house full of baby stuff again if things go wrong." It was incredibly hard to look at all the things Tanner had gotten for Daniel. I know I told Tanner I was going to get rid of them, but I never got around to doing it before I lost him.

I had Quinn bring it all to goodwill. I can't believe she doesn't remember how hard that was for me. She couldn't possibly expect me to allow that to happen again!

"But you already painted the nursery and have been looking at furniture," she says.

I sigh. "Yes, I did. But that is different than having a party where people bring boat loads of gifts. What if something happens? I don't want to face all those people again if things go badly. Celebrating a baby that I'm not guaranteed isn't something I'm interested in…"

"Quinn, you're not going to change her mind," Tanner says as he emerges from the house with a new round of drinks for everyone. Beer for him. Martini for Quinn and cranberry juice for me. It'd be nice if I could add some vodka to it for this conversation. Quinn means well, but she just doesn't understand my fear of jinxing this pregnancy. I'm almost done. Nine more weeks left. I made it this far. I will let nothing get in the way of me bringing home a healthy baby. Even if that makes me a superstitious weirdo.

Shaking her head, it's now her turn to sigh. "I just don't get it. Isn't this what all first moms get all excited over? I don't want you to regret not having one and then blame me for not pushing you harder."

"I don't need you to understand. I just need you to respect my wishes," I say grabbing her hand with a smile. "I won't regret this and I certainly wouldn't blame you."

"I wish I knew this before I researched all that baby shower shit. Those are hours of my life I'll never get back," she retorts before downing the drink Tanner placed in front of her.

"ARE YOU SURE this is how you want to spend your first Mother's Day?" Tanner asks as he enters the kitchen.

"This technically isn't my first mother's day. The baby isn't here yet so I'm not really a mom yet," I explain, again, while I finish signing the cards I got for his mother and sisters.

"Yes, you are. Stop with that nonsense," he says wrapping his arms around me from behind. I love when he does this. It makes me feel all warm and fuzzy. I'm thanking all these hormones for this extra sentimentalism I'm feeling.

I told Quinn and Tanner rather than a baby shower, I'd prefer celebrating our daughter with a Mother's Day dinner. Quinn has been harping on me that I'm being ridiculous, thinking that having a shower is going to jinx anything but too damn bad. This is what I want. Besides, Tanner and I couldn't agree on anything for the nursery. He wants this crazy princess castle bed. Yes, bed not crib. Bed. Needless to say, I'll be the one ordering all the furniture for the baby.

"You sure you still don't want to call your mom and invite her over?" he asks for the millionth time since I started planning this dinner.

"Why? So she can tell me that I'm doing everything wrong. I'm happy. I love my life. I love everything we've built together. I don't need my mother here to tell me what she feels I'm doing wrong or what can be improved. No. No, thank you."

"She's still your mom, Ashley," he says as if that's supposed to make me see reason. It does but not in the way he thinks.

"All she's ever given me, besides life, is the perfect example of the type of mother I don't ever want to be," I tell him, collecting the cards and placing them in front of the flowers I got for each of them.

I should have known Tanner would be right behind me, "I didn't mean to upset you. I just don't want you to look back and have regrets. I've loved sharing this experience with my parents."

"If I had parents like yours, I'm sure I would too."

Dinner is supposed to start at five and Quinn promised to come by at four to help get everything ready. It's four-thirty and she's still not here, so I'm running around trying to make sure that everything is all set up.

"I told you to let me hire servers for tonight, but no. You said you wanted to do it yourself," he says taking the large floral centerpiece from my hands and carrying it over to the dining room table.

"Well, Quinn was supposed to be here already but I guess she got held up at her parents. And I let you have it catered, so shut up," I glare at him.

"We both know why it was catered, Ash and it wasn't because you allowed me to do it," he retorts with a smug smirk. Everyone knows I'm a terrible cook.

I don't get to zing him back with some smart ass comment because Quinn comes barreling through the door, making a grand entrance as always.

"Sorry, I'm late. I could have been here earlier, but I figured murdering my parents on a holiday specifically for one of them, might be frowned upon." There's a bunch of rustling in the kitchen before she meets us in the dining room.

"What happened now?" I ask taking in her frazzled state.

"An ambush. They decided it was the perfect time to set a luncheon with Jordan's family to press me further on this stupid merger. But I don't want to talk about it so what can I help you with?" she asks as she kicks her heels into the corner of the room.

Half an hour later, Tanner's family has all arrived and we are settled outside by the pool enjoying the beautiful weather. This is my idea of a perfect family day. Sunshine, smiles, and love.

"Can we give Aunt Ashley her presents, now?" Veronica's youngest daughter, Nicole, asks.

"Presents?" *What the heck is she talking about?*

"Sure. Let's get them from the garage." Veronica grabs Nicole and Maci and heads inside.

"I know you didn't want a shower, but did you really think that we wouldn't get anything for that little lady you've got in there?"

Margaret smiles at me as Veronica and the girls emerge from the house with tons of pink and purple gift bags.

I'm knee deep in bags filled with adorable little outfits for the baby, including the cutest little Jets cheerleading outfit courtesy of her big cousins.

"You guys didn't have to do this," I smile, tears welling in my eyes.

"Of course, we did," all the women say in unison.

"And this one is from me," Tanner says handing me a small, pink wrapped box.

I smile wondering how the hell I got so lucky marrying into such a wonderful family as I open the gift from Tanner.

The tears flow freely as I take in the new charm for my charm bracelet. It's a beautiful mother-child charm. The image of the mother wrapped around a small child.

"Turn it over," Tanner instructs wearing a smile of his own.

A mother holds her child forever

I don't try to contain my tears any longer.

"It's beautiful." My life is beautiful and all because of this man.

Best "technically not" first Mother's day ever.

Chapter Fifteen

TANNER

TIME HAS FLOWN by. Ashley's due in exactly one month. ONE freaking month until Ashley and I become parents. It didn't really hit me until this morning. As we were getting ready to head over to my parents for their Father's Day barbecue, it dawned on me that this will be the last year I'm just celebrating my own father. Next year I'll be celebrating the miracle of being a dad myself.

Standing here watching my father with my nieces and nephew, I hope like hell I'll be half the dad that man is. I can't remember a time when my dad didn't have my back, even when he wasn't happy with the things I've done. My huge fuck up with Ashley comes to mind. Even though he didn't agree with what I had done, he never judged me. He listened to me and gave me his best advice. What more can you ask for in a father? I've had a great example, just as Alex pointed out when I tried to convince myself Ashley was trying to trap me. I just hope I live up to his example.

"What are you doing over here all by yourself?" Alex asks, handing me a beer. Speak of the devil.

"Just taking everything in. Everything in my life is about to change and I can't help but think I won't live up to my father's expectations as a dad. He's a damn good dad. What if I'm not as good at it as he is?" I ask as I chug a little of the beer Alex just handed me.

"You'll do fine. Plus, the old man is still around. You can still go to him for advice," he smiles making a very good point.

"True. I wish you were going to be around more. I hate having my main man across the country." I hate having 'my person' three time zones away. Fuck, Ashley has me watching too much *Grey's Anatomy* if I'm referring to Alex as my person now.

"Well," he says sheepishly. "You know Art's retiring, right?"

"Yeah, we're going to miss him. He ran a tight ship and was one of the best trainers I've ever worked with, no offense." I think I can see where this is going, but I don't want to get my hopes up.

"None taken. He's damn good at what he does and they've asked me to be his replacement. You could be looking at the new head trainer of the Jets," he says very nonchalantly.

"What do you mean *could* be?" Unless… "Was the offer not good enough?"

"Nah, the offer was definitely worth the move back," he explains but now I'm even more confused.

"So, what's the holdup?"

"I'm just not sure if it's the right move for me right now." His face shows a hint of sadness and I have a feeling as to why. He only gets that look when someone mentions Quinn.

"Does this have anything to do with Quinn?" I ask the million dollar question.

"No… Yes…Hell, I don't know," he says running his hand through his hair in aggravation. "All I know is that I don't know what the hell

I want to do. They gave me time to consider it so that's what I'm doing."

I don't press him for anything more. Now's not the time. Now's the time to show him what he's missing here: *family*.

Everyone spends the next few hours with a belly full of food and smiles on their faces. Family. This is what everything is all about in life. There's nothing greater. Not winning the Super Bowl. Not having a padded bank account. Not fancy cars or a huge house. I feel sorry for those who don't have what I have. This, right here, is more than enough. Life. Love. Blessings. I just wish that I could give this to those that mean this much to me who don't have it.

"DID YOU ENJOY your first father's day? Even though it's not really your first." Ashley asks on the way home from my parents. She couldn't resist throwing that last part in.

Smiling at her, I reach over to wrap my hand around hers and give it a squeeze. "I did."

"I'm glad. It's crazy how much everything's going to change soon," she says mirroring my thoughts from earlier.

"Speaking of changes," I say. "Alex just told me that we offered him Art's position."

"Oh my god," she squeals in excitement. "He'll be back on this coast just in time for all the baby stuff."

"Well..." *How do I break this to her?* "He hasn't decided yet if he's going to take it."

"What? Why on Earth wouldn't he?" she asks confused.

"Well..." I start, trying to think of how to explain to her how Alex is feeling. It sucks being in the middle of our best friends. Alex isn't just my best friend, he's become one of Ashley's over the years as well. The same for Quinn and I, she is one of my best friends now, too. His leaving was hard on Ash. It was hard for me too. He'd become very instrumental to Ashley in her recovery. They spent a lot of time together working on her knee and arm. It took almost a year for her to get back to normal. Well, as normal as you can get after everything her body went through. All those hours together bonded them in a way I didn't know possible. They'd become just as close as he and I were. The same went for me and Quinn. All those days I spent at their condo forged a bond between us too.

"Quinn? Right?" she sighs. I just nod my head. "Fucking Quinn. I'm starting to wish those two never hooked up to begin with. Her foolishness is hurting everyone but her. She has to be the reason things went south between the two of them. I just wish I knew what the hell happened so I can smack some sense into her."

"You and me both, baby," I agree. "You and me both."

"Do you think we could talk him into it?" she asks a little too hopeful.

"We could, but I don't think that is a good idea."

"Why the hell not? Don't you miss him?" Her tone shocked as if I just insulted him or something.

"Of course, I do, but I don't want to press him into making a decision he could come to regret. He needs to do what's right for him and him alone. We can't be selfish here. What if he takes the job, and he's miserable and then he resents us? I'd rather him be on the other side of the country than cause him more pain when it comes to this whole mess." She needs to understand this isn't about us.

"I hate it when you make a good point," she huffs clearly annoyed because she knows I am right.

"How about I show you how good my point is when we get home? You didn't happen to get yourself one of those cheerleading outfits as a present for me, did you?" I smirk knowing damn well that promises of sex will most definitely turn Ashley's mood from sad to happy in a heartbeat.

Chapter Sixteen

ASHLEY

LEAVING MY DOCTOR'S appointment this morning, I'm not a happy camper. Today's my due date and my darling little daughter doesn't seem to have any plans of making her entrance into the world today. Dr. Marcus' words echo in my head causing me further disappointment.

"You're not dilated at all Ashley. Looks like this little one has no intentions of coming today."

He offered to schedule an induction for me, but I don't want that. I don't want any medical intervention in evicting this baby from my belly unless I have no other choice. I'm not opting for an epidural either, much to Tanner's dismay. He says he doesn't think he'll be able to see me in that pain, but he doesn't understand this isn't about me. I won't do anything that could potentially harm my baby just to ease my discomfort, including being induced.

I will, on the other hand, follow the doctor's suggestions to help jump start labor.

Exercise, spicy food, and sex. Yes, my husband will be getting laid more than a mattress.

"She'll come when she's ready, baby," Tanner says trying to make me feel better. Too bad for me there is no making me feel better until this baby decides it's time to get the hell out. Now I know how Rachel felt during that episode of *Friends*. It's like a hundred degrees and clothing should be optional, pregnant or not.

"Stop for some Indian takeout on the way home, please," I request. Step one in operation 'Let's have a baby'.

"Indian?" he questions. In his defense, I don't request Indian often.

"Can you think of anything spicier than Indian food?" I ask with a raised eyebrow.

"Ahh, I see. Going to be trying out all the doctor's suggestions?" he smirks annoyingly. I like how he gets all of the benefits of having a child with none of the work or discomforts. Little does he know, he will be making that fact up to me with lots of middle of the night diaper changes.

"Yes, and I plan on getting my exercise later while doing squats over your cock," I throw back at him.

"You think, huh?" he says wearing that stupid, smug smirk of his.

"Oh, I know," I state matter-of-factly. "You're going to spend the day fucking your daughter out of me."

"That has to be the worst dirty talk in the history of dirty talk. That's all kind of fucked up sounding, Ashley," he points out with a disturbed look on his face.

"Oh, shut up and drive the damn car." I'm in no mood for him to get all bent out of shape over some stupid words. He's going to fuck me whether he likes the reason or not.

There's only room for one of us to be temperamental right now and it's me.

"You ordering me around is kinda hot."

ALL THE INDIAN food did was give me heartburn, so I decide a hot shower might help. It doesn't. I don't know why I thought a hot shower in the middle of July was the answer, but all it does is make me irritable. So irritable that I didn't even hear Tanner come up behind me while I scowl at all the clothes in the closet.

Wrapping his arms around me to rub my belly, he kisses my neck and asks, "What's with the face?"

"I hate all these clothes," I pout. "I don't want to wear any of them."

"So don't. All they're going to do is get in my way of getting to this," he points out while he dips his hands lower to play with my clit.

Reaching around, I rub his hardness through his pants and agree. "Good point. Why don't you distract me from my terrible mood with this magnificent cock of yours?"

Tanner lets out a deep chuckle before thrusting one long, thick finger into my pussy. "Challenge accepted. Hope I can use more than my cock."

The moan slips right passed my lips and my fingers squeeze tighter around his thick cock. "Please, do. You may use every talent in your very skilled repertoire."

"Oh, don't you worry, I will," he forewarns before removing his fingers from my core, much to my dismay.

"Quit your whining and get that ass on the bed like a good little girl," he admonishes, smacking me on the ass.

I run to the bed as fast as a nine-month pregnant woman can run and lay in the middle. Not only can this jump start labor, but there is nothing better than getting lost in my husband. Sometimes I think the man was made specifically just to please me.

"Show me my pretty pussy, Ashley," Tanner demands when he reaches the side of the bed. I bend my legs and spread them open for him to see.

"So pink and wet," hc says before grabbing my ankles and dragging me to the end of the bed.

My entire body quivers with anticipation as I watch Tanner drops to his knees in front of me. He runs his nose along my inner thigh. "You have no idea what the smell of your arousal does to me." He gives me one long, slow lick from top to bottom before he sucks my clit into his mouth.

"Mmm…" I moan as Tanner's tongue glides through me top to bottom in one long savoring lick. It feels so incredibly good.

From everything I've read online, most women don't want to have sex this late into their pregnancy but I can't seem to get enough of Tanner. Watching him take out the trash has me incredibly turned on lately.

"Up," he orders as he gets naked faster than a virgin on prom night. "I want you to sit on my face, baby."

Fuck! The shit this man says. This has been one of his new favorite things since we've had to become a little more creative in our play time. A giant belly tends to be a bit restrictive.

"Now!" He shouts as he climbs up the bed and lays flat on his back. "Don't make me tell you again." Have I mentioned that I've started to enjoy his domineering ways even more now? And Tanner knows it.

"I'm coming," I reply as I crawl my way over his body.

"Not yet, but you will be. Repeatedly." As if I wasn't wet enough before. I straddle his face as requested and grab onto the headboard for support. I know he's going to rock my world the minute he gets that wicked tongue on me.

Tanner wastes no time diving into action. My eyes roll back and I moan loudly as he hits my sweet spot. This man and his knowledge of my body are something to never be taken for granted. My hips agree with my brain as they rock on his face all on their own.

"Yes, just like that, baby. Ride my tongue," he growls against my already sensitive flesh. Fuck! I can't tell if the first orgasm ended and another began, or if this is just one long fantastic orgasm.

As my body finally stops undulating, Tanner kisses my slit softly and says, "Christ that was the hottest thing I've ever seen you do. I need to be inside you. Like right now!"

I slide my body down his until I'm sitting on his engorged cock. I slick it with my wetness as I grind back and forth on him. "Can't take much of that, baby," he groans.

Reaching between us, I grab hold of him, lining us up, then sink down onto him, eliciting the most erotic moan from him that I've ever heard.

"How the hell do you keep getting tighter? Fuck, you fit me like a glove," he announces, matching my earlier sentiments of him being made to please me.

"And you feel huge," I pant. "There's no better feeling in the world than this right here."

"Ride me, baby," he orders, gripping my hips and directing my movements. I only last a few minutes before my larger than normal body protests against my delight. My thighs start cramping and I'm out of breath. You'd think I was running a marathon as opposed to having great sex with my husband. But then again sex with Tanner has always been the best work out.

"Need to switch positions, baby?" he questions. As always, he is so totally in tune with me.

Nodding my head, I unseat myself from him and stand on the side of the bed.

"Gentle now?" he asks as I bend over the bed.

"Hell no! I just couldn't keep up the pace. Don't you dare go soft on me now!" I demand.

"With you bent over and this glorious ass on display, there's no way I'd ever go soft," he snorts in amusement, stroking his cock.

"I wasn't talking about your dick and you know it, now please fuck me," I grumble, annoyed he can find anything amusing at the moment. I stay bent over the bed, not patiently waiting to be taken on a good ride. My husband stands behind me, his dick in hand, laughing.

My husband lets out a hushed laugh as he steps behind me, dick in his hand. "Far be it for me to deny my needy wife," he proclaims before impaling me with his cock much slower than I'd like.

I growl in frustration. "Harder, Tanner."

"I'm not fucking you like a dirty whore right now, Ashley. I know you're on a mission but I will fuck you how I want to fuck you. And you will like whatever it is that I give you." he grunts, slapping my ass as a reprimand.

"Well, feel free to start giving it." I goad him.

"Don't make me gag you!"

Twenty minutes and two orgasms later, we both lay sated on the bed. "Was that good enough for you?" he inquires between gasps for air.

"Since I don't feel any different than an hour ago, no it wasn't good enough for me," I bitch. You'd think three orgasms would make me a little less irate but alas, it doesn't.

"I'm pretty sure it doesn't happen instantly, Ash. We can always go again," he suggests, that fucking chuckle back in his voice.

"No. I don't want to go again." I whine like a child told she can't have any more dessert. Well, I guess I was told I can't have any dessert since my husband has now gone to the boring side.

"Why not?" he asks sounding slightly insulted.

"Because you won't fuck me like I want to be fucked. I want you to fuck me like I'm not made of glass. Christ, how hard is it to understand!"

"You're nine months pregnant, I'm not going to fuck you like we're making a porn, Ashley."

"What if I let you tape it?" That should be more than an incentive. I mean what guy doesn't want to make a home video

"Nope," he shakes his head refusing to bite the bait.

"Well, fine then. I'll go get Fake Tanner. I bet I can make him fuck me hard." I threaten hoping that bringing up my vibrator will spur him into action. I'm almost out of tricks.

"You pull out that vibrator and I'm telling you right now, you won't be able to sit for a week. And not because I fucked your brains out. That's a promise," he retorts. The glare he is throwing at me definitely means he's not kidding.

"Hmph," I grumble, getting out of bed to head to the bathroom. I slam the door hard enough to let my husband know he's in the doghouse.

Chapter Seventeen

TANNER

"**WHAT TIME ARE** you leaving?" Ashley asks as she waddles into the kitchen. Yes, waddles. I feel so bad for her. I wish I could do something for her, but I've learned over the last week that nothing I do will help ease her discomfort any less. I just keep my mouth shut and do as I'm told. Except for making love to my wife like she wants. She's still pretty pissed that I won't get rough with her, but that's too damn bad.

"Alex is on his way here now. As soon as he gets here, we'll head out. We shouldn't be gone too long. You sure you're going to be okay while I'm gone?" I'm not entirely comfortable leaving her alone, but we've been attached at the hip lately. We're starting to get on each other's nerves at this point. Turns out, there is such a thing as too much togetherness.

With the season about to start, I would've liked to spend this time with our new daughter. Since that doesn't seem to be happening according to plan, I'll settle for being happy with my wife. But with her being nine months pregnant and hating the world at the moment, it hasn't been an easy task.

"I'll be fine. Quinn texted a little bit ago saying she's going to stop by later. Apparently, she has something to tell me. So I won't be alone long. Besides, I can't wait to see what your dad has done with that old rocking chair."

My dad refinished the old rocking chair that used to be in my room as a child for Ash to put in the nursery. I told her I'd gladly get her a more modern one, but she refused, insisting things with sentimental value were far better than anything new.

"You know," she sighs. "I really miss having Alex around. Has he told you yet if he's going to take the job you guys offered him? Training camp starts next week. I'd assume he has to make a decision soon."

"He hasn't said anything to me, but I feel like he was leaning toward it. I'm going to see if I can push him on an answer today." I'd love not needing to board a plane to see my best friend.

"Okay, use the powers of suggestion you always use on me. Lord knows I can't seem to ever tell you no," she giggles for what seems like the first time in days.

"I don't think Alex is interested in my dick, baby." I point out causing a smile to spread across her face. God, it's so good to see more than a frown on her face.

"True. But it is a fabulous dick," she says as she wraps her arms around me and kisses my neck.

"Come on, don't you two ever stop that shit?" Alex asks from the garage entrance at the other end of the kitchen.

"That's what you get when you don't knock like regular people," I smirk at him. I've really missed his smartass around here too.

"You don't seem too interested in keeping people out if you still have the same alarm code," he smirks as he comes around to wrap his arms around my wife, who is overjoyed to see him.

"Alex!" she shrieks. "I've missed you so much."

"You look beautiful, Ashley. When is this little beauty going to make her appearance?" he asks rubbing her very large belly.

"Three weeks ago would have been good." Ashley smiles luminously at him. Now if I had asked that question, she would have thrown the closest heavy object at my head.

"Okay, Romeo, you ready to head out?" I ask, interrupting his quality time with my wife. I'm a little irked that she's all smiles with him and I can't even breathe right in her presence anymore.

"Yeah. You want to take my truck since it will be easier than yours?" Thank god one of us is using his brain. I didn't even think about how'd I try to fit the chair in my Cayenne since Ashley now drives my Rover. Nothing fits in that damn SUV. That's the last impulse buy I let Ashley talk me into.

"Yeah, that'd be a smart plan," I answer him, pulling Ashley away from him and into my arms. "I'll be back later. Be a good girl."

"Yeah, because I can get into a whole lot of trouble toting this big thing around with me," she quips pointing to her belly.

I BREATHE OUT a sigh of relief when we pull out of the driveway.

"You okay?" Alex asks.

"Yeah, it's just nice to have some guy time, you know? Don't get me wrong, I love Ashley, but everything I do lately seems to piss her off. So for the next few hours, at least I don't have to watch my every move afraid I'm going to do something else to make her mad." I sigh. I love her more than life itself, I do, but fuck if it isn't nice to breathe a little easier right now.

"She seemed fine to me," he laughs. *Bastard.*

"Yeah, because you didn't knock her up. And she misses you," I point out. "I miss you, man."

"I miss you guys too," he admits sadly.

"Does that mean you're going to accept the job?" I ask.

"I love it in Arizona, but it's not home you know? Things aren't the same when you don't have the people you care about around."

"And by people you care about, do you mean us or Quinn?" I question. I wish he'd give me little more to go on about what happened with them.

His voice turns from sad to hard with each word that passes his lips. "You guys. It's hard to care about people that don't care about you."

"Well, sometimes it's hard to show people you care about them from the other side of the country," I say raising an eyebrow.

An unhappy look overtakes Alex's face and his body language screams out his dislike for our topic of conversation. "I loved that girl. The lack of caring didn't come from me," he says harshly.

In all the years I've known this man, I've seen him truly this upset over something. Whatever happened between the had to really gut him. "How was I supposed to know that, man? It's not like you ever told me what happened with you two," I push to see if he'll cave and finally let us know what really went down with them.

"Fuck, I don't even know what happened with us!" he shouts, finally losing what little composure he was holding onto. "Everything was great and then boom, she wants nothing to do with me. That's all the explanation I got. Even when I pressed for more, she shut down. She quit us cold turkey. We were together for almost two years and then done. That's it. What the hell is anyone supposed to make of that?"

Damn, I never thought it went down like that. No wonder he doesn't want to talk about. "I'm sorry. That has to be rough." I say. At least when Ashley left my stupid ass I knew why, and I as able to fight my way through trying to fix it.

"You're telling me? I fucked my way through half of Phoenix, and I still can't get that woman out of my head."

I can't help but laugh at his statement. At least he still can make a joke about it. "Does any of that mean you're coming home?" I ask.

He runs his hands through his hair and sighs, "I took the job two weeks ago. I just haven't said anything yet because I'm still not sure if it's the right choice for me."

"Well, since you took the job. No turning back now. If you couldn't fuck her out of your head from across the country, then I say coming home where you have support is a good choice." My opinion may be biased, but I'm fucking stoked that he'll be back here with us and just in time for the baby.

"Yeah, but she'll be here too," he says.

"So, I guess now would be a bad time to tell you that Ashley and I would like you to be the baby's godfather?"

"Why would it be a bad time? That's a great thing. I'd be honored." He exclaims with a huge smile on his face.

"Because Ashley is asking Quinn to be the godmother," I sigh.

"Fuck," he says. "Well, fuck her. I'm not going to let her ruin this honor for me."

I hope he's right. I hope these two can work their shit out. For themselves and for all of us.

"You may have to cut your hair, though," I smirk, trying to lighten the mood. "The long haired surfer boy thing doesn't work so well on the East Coast."

Grabbing the ridiculous bun thing on the top of his head, he grins. "I'm not cutting shit. The ladies love this hair."

Chapter Eighteen

ASHLEY

"**YOU DID WHAT?"** I screech unable to control myself. "Have you lost your mind?" I pace the length of my living room shaking my head back and forth as if it will expel the ridiculousness that just left Quinn's mouth.

"It really isn't that big of a deal, Ash," she sighs. "It was inevitable. I don't know why I bothered to fight it for so long. I kind of feel like a weight has been lifted off my shoulders now that I gave in."

"Not a big deal? It's a huge fucking deal! Like monumental! Like on a crazy scale of one to ten, this ranks four-thousand-thirty-seven! How can you not see that this is exactly what you have always been trying to avoid?" I yell at her. I can feel the heat radiating off my face, I'm that angry. I can hear the blood rushing in my ears and my legs are pacing extremely fast for a woman who is one week overdue.

"You need to calm yourself down. It's already done. I don't need your over-protective husband to walk through the door, see you pacing like a madwoman, and rip me a new asshole for you going off the deep end." Her voice is calm, almost defeated. I have never seen Quinn like this. I just can't wrap my head around it. How can she be okay with this bullshit farce? Someone needs to knock some sense into her.

"Is it my turn to bitch slap some sense into you? I've been waiting over three years for my turn," I ask, redirecting my energy from pacing to cornering my idiotic best friend. Raising my hand, I mimic a slapping motion. "I've got plenty of baby powder. We can make this authentic to ensure I get my point across." I laugh because let's face it, picturing myself bitch slapping Quinn, pimp style, is pretty fucking funny.

"Do you have baby wipes to go with that baby powder, because I'm pretty sure you just pissed yourself," she laughs. "You're not very intimidating when you're standing in a puddle of pee, bitch."

"I didn't pee," I say. My voice is entirely too calm for someone who just realized her water has broken.

"Please don't tell me that is what I think it is then?" she says, the tone of her voice disgusted and panicked.

I stare down at the puddle of fluids surrounding my feet and my mind goes blank. "It is," I tell her, starting to feel slightly panicked myself.

There are a million things I should be doing right now but I can't focus on anything other than the fact my water has broken in my living room. My water is supposed to break after I get to the hospital. After I'm settled in and being monitored by medical professionals. In a hospital where there's less of a chance anything could go wrong. Why aren't I feeling contractions? I should be feeling contractions which must mean something's definitely wrong.

"Sweets, you're white as a ghost. What should we be doing right now? I know I don't know much about childbirth, but I'm pretty sure that when your water breaks, you should definitely be heading to the hospital." Quinn says drawing my attention away from the mess on the floor.

The only thing I seem to be able to do is stare at her blankly. I can't move. I'm frozen with fear. Fear that I'm going to go through the same experience again. Fear that I will head into the hospital with a healthy baby in my belly and leave with nothing but heartbreak. I know without a doubt there is no way I could handle that again. It would break me. I would never come back from it. God wouldn't be that cruel would he? I've had an amazing three years. Sure it was a struggle but I'm happy now. I deserve to be happy. Tanner deserves to be happy. We deserve to be parents. God wouldn't do this to us again. Right?

Quinn's voice breaks through my haze. "What am I supposed to do? She's just standing there like a statue." It must be Tanner since I'm pretty sure she doesn't have my OB's phone number in her phone. "Okay. Okay. Here she is."

I take the phone from Quinn's outstretched hand and bring it to my ear. I just hold it there and breathe because I don't know how to tell Tanner I think something is horribly wrong. I haven't felt the baby move. I haven't felt a contraction. As long as I stand here in my home, there's no doctor to tell me for sure that my greatest fear is about to happen again. It feels like Daniel all over again. Everything was fine until it wasn't.

"Baby, I can hear you breathing. What's going on? Talk to me, please." The pleading tone in his voice begs me to tell him everything's fine. Begging for me to tell him everything will be okay, and I can't. I can't do that. Because I don't feel like everything is fine.

"There's no contractions," I whisper, as though whispering is better than saying the words at normal volume. "There should be contractions, but there's not. I don't feel her moving either. Something's wrong." I surprise myself when my voice doesn't catch and my lips don't quiver.

"I'm sure there's nothing wrong, baby. Everything's been one hundred percent fine the entire pregnancy. You're just scared, which is okay. Everything's going to be fine. I need you to call Dr. Marcus. You need to tell him what's going on and do what he says. I'm going to get in the car now and head back toward home. Call me back after you talk to the doctor and let me know what's going on? Can you do that for me, baby? I promise you everything will be okay." The even and reassuring tone of Tanner's voice washes over me, helping to calm my racing mind.

"Okay," I tell him, knowing I need to do what he's asking. I can't stand here and expect everything to just work itself out. I need to get to the hospital.

"Okay. I love you, Ashley. Everything will be perfectly fine," he says confidently. God, I hope he's right.

Chapter Nineteen

TANNER

"I LOVE YOU, TOO. Please hurry," she whispers. The fear in her voice is evident and my heart breaks for her. She's been semi-neurotic this entire pregnancy. I can't fully blame her. There have been times I've been just as bad, but I, at least, have enjoyed the miraculous journey of watching our precious daughter grow within Ash. She's been so riddled with worry and concern, she hasn't given herself the chance to enjoy the gift we've been given.

"I'm on my way. Stay strong." I tell her before disconnecting the call and turning to see three sets of eyes staring at me.

"Well, is it time?" Ma asks having heard enough of my conversation to know I was just talking to Ashley and it has to do with the baby.

"Her water just broke. She's a mess, though. She said she isn't feeling contractions and has now convinced herself something is wrong," I explain while heading to the counter to grab Alex's keys and my sunglasses. "We gotta head out. I'll call you with more info when I hear back from Ash." I kiss Ma on the cheek and clap my dad on the back before whistling at Alex, "Move your ass, dude. I'm about to become a daddy."

"Yeah, sure. You can drive my car," he laughs as we head out the door.

We're about ten minutes into our drive back to Jersey when Ashley calls back. "What did the doctor say, baby?" I ask in a smooth calm voice, knowing that Ash is probably still freaked out.

"He said to head over to the hospital, even though I'm not feeling any contractions. He said they'll start soon. I also felt her move a little bit, but I'm still worried." She sounds less anxious than she did before, which makes me relax a little more. I don't like when Ash is stressed and I'm not there to comfort her. That's my only role in this whole process. Be there for Ashley. Anything she wants, she gets. Of course, my darling little princess had to decide to start her entrance while I'm an hour away in the next state. Thankfully, this pregnancy timed well with the beginning of the season and training camp. I've gotten to be here with Ash instead of away upstate. A few weeks later and I would've had to leave for camp with a very pregnant wife alone at home. I don't know how I would've left her for days at a time, needing an airplane to get back to her. Been there. Done that. Never want to experience it again.

"You already have your bag in the car. Have Quinn drive you and I will meet you there. I'm already on my way back. I'll be there before you know it. See you in forty-five minutes, baby. I love you. Everything is going to be okay." I'm rambling, but I'm trying my best to soothe her. And myself if I'm honest. I wish I was there with her.

"Okay. Please hurry. I'm scared." The sound of her voice reminds me of a small child who's lost their mom in a department store.

My foot presses down a little harder on the gas pedal as I tell her, "I'm coming, baby. I'm coming."

I make great timing on my way out of Staten Island until we get over the bridge and 440 is a damn parking lot. "You've got to be fucking kidding me!" I yell out, slamming my fist down into the steering wheel.

"Let me see if I can find out what's going on," Alex says, his hand already on the radio switching to the traffic report stations. He scans until we hear a traffic report mention the 440 jam.

"An overturned tractor trailer is holding up traffic between the Goethals and Bayonne Bridge. Expect about an hour delay if you're heading that way."

Motherfucker! I don't have an hour to be sitting here in traffic! I have a very frightened wife in labor that needs me now!

"See if you can find another route," I snap, taking my frustration out on Alex.

"You know we need to hit the bridge in order to get there, there is no other way. It's only two miles maybe it won't be too bad."

He's right. There is no other way to get where we're going at this point, but I don't believe for a second that it won't be too bad. The fucking highway is at a goddamn stand still.

We just sit in the car for what feels like an eternity. I glance at the clock and realize it's only be fifteen minutes. *How the hell has it only been fifteen minutes?* The shitty talk radio station hasn't given any more information on the traffic jam and it's pissing me off. Any other day, they wouldn't be shutting up about an accident causing major delays. Alex doesn't speak to me and I don't speak to him. He knows me well enough to know I don't want to talk. My mind is racing with thoughts of not being there for Ashley when she needs me, a second time.

Katy Perry's *Unconditionally* breaks through my ugly thoughts. It also sends my heart racing knowing it's my ring tone for Ashley. I'm going to have to tell her it's going to be longer than expected before I can get to her. I can't help the feeling of déjà vu that surrounds me. Ashley needs me and I'm not there for her. Again.

"Hello?"

"Please tell me that you're almost here, shit's gone crazy over here." Quinn's voice was not the one that I was expecting. The fact that she's saying things aren't going well does nothing to help me in my current situation. I feel utterly helpless.

"What do you…" I don't get to finish my question because Ash lets out a blood-curdling scream. My heart stops beating and my blood turns cold. A scream like that can mean nothing good.

Chapter Twenty

ASHLEY

"**WHERE IS HE?"** I ask between gritted teeth. *Fuck this shit hurts!* I liked it better when the contractions weren't coming. *Why didn't anyone warn me it hurts this fucking much?* Probably because people will stop having kids! I don't think I will ever want to experience this again. Even as I think it, I know I'm full of shit. No matter how much this shit hurts, if it gets me my precious daughter, I'd do it over and over again. The only thing I need right now is my damn husband.

"We just got to the hospital, we're waiting for them to get her a wheelchair and then they're taking her to her room. The doctor called ahead for her, so her room is ready. Where are you?" Quinn explains.

"There's an accident on 440 and he's stuck in traffic," Quinn tells me. The fear evident in her eyes, she is terrified of me right now. I can't blame her. I think I made her bleed before when I grabbed her hand and squeezed it through my first contraction. They started about twenty minutes ago, out of nowhere. There was no easing into them. They came fast and strong without much of a break between them. I thought you were supposed to get an introductory period before they made you want to die.

"What the fuck do you mean he's stuck in traffic? He's supposed to be here with me. I can't do this without him." I don't get to say anything before another contraction hits me hard. I try to breathe through it but that shit they teach you in Lamaze doesn't work for shit. I can't focus on anything other than the pain.

"Give me the phone." I reach my hand out and take the phone from Quinn just as the orderly, who left to get a wheelchair, rounds the corner with it.

"Have a seat and I'll get you up to L&D and you can get settled in," he says with a smile on his face. I want to smack that smile right off his face. With my husband's arrival unknown at this point, I can do nothing but scowl. And this guy's smiling face just makes me more irritated.

"I won't be able to settle in until my husband gets here," I growl at the orderly as he's pushing my wheelchair into the elevator. My comment was directed to Tanner. I know he heard me because I made sure to say it into the phone. "How much longer Tanner?" The change in the tone of my voice is noticeable. As the contraction ebbs, I feel less hostile.

"I'm trying my hardest, Ashley. 440 is barely moving. The reports on the radio just said that they've finished clearing the mess up, but I don't have a definitive time for you. I wish I did. I'm doing the best I can." He sounds utterly defeated. Thoughts of the past, images of him in Miami getting the call, needing a plane to get to me, flash through my mind. This has to be hard for him too. Possibly worse this time because he's so close yet so far.

"I know you are. I just need youuuuu…" Another contraction hits, harder this time than all the last, and I don't get to finish my thought.

"Ash…baby…breathe. You can do this. I know you can. I love you. You can do this." He says a few other things, but I don't hear the words, just his voice. His voice calms me.

By the time the contraction ends, I'm in my room. A nurse comes in and tells me to remove this and change into that. "Hurry…" I plead with him before handing the phone back to Quinn while I take the gown from the nurse and head into the en-suite bathroom to change.

Fifteen minutes later, I'm lying in an uncomfortable hospital bed with bands wrapped around my belly monitoring the baby and me. I'm waiting for Dr. Marcus to come in and check me.

Another contraction hits hard as my doctor enters the room. *Oh my God.* My fingers are wrapped so tightly around the bed rails that I'm sure I hear it crack. I feel like I'm going to hyperventilate as I breathe through this one. I swear it feels like it's never going to end. They keep getting stronger and lasting longer.

"Longer, deeper breaths, Ashley. You're going to make yourself dizzy and lightheaded if you keep breathing like that," he says as he sits on the end of the bed and flings the blankets up off my legs. "I'm going to check your progress as soon as that contraction ends. It's almost done." *How the hell could he possibly know when this contraction is going to end?*

"I can see it on the monitor," he says answering my unspoken question.

He rips open a little foil packet of what looks like lube and coats his fingers before looking up at me and asking, "You ready? This is going to be uncomfortable." He doesn't wait for me to answer before he inserts said fingers in me and starts moving them in deep places that shouldn't ever be provoked while your body is trying to expel another human being.

"HOLY SHIT!" I yell. I'm doing my best to try and crawl up the bed and away from him. This is by far one of the most painful things I've ever felt.

"I know, sweetie, I know. I need you to hang in there just another second or two, okay?" he asks continuing to dig around in my vagina. "You're just about six centimeters."

I'm absolutely floored that I'm that far along already. "SIX? I thought that it was supposed to be a longer process?" I ask.

He pulls the papers coming from the monitoring machine out and reads the graph things on them. "Yes, six. Every woman is different, so each labor is different. It's not the same every time. Sometimes it's twenty-four hours and sometimes it's four. There's never any way to predict each labor. Do you want to have an epidural, Ashley?"

"No, I don't want any drugs," I answer.

"Okay, let me know if you change your mind. Things are going to get very intense soon." He smiles, nods his head and leaves the room.

I grab my phone to call Tanner. He answers immediately and I begin freaking out. "Where the hell are you? The doctor just checked me and I'm six centimeters already, Tanner! SIX! I need you now! You promised me that you would be here for everything." In reality, I know yelling and screaming at Tanner isn't going to make him get here any faster but I'm not thinking rationally right now.

"I can see my exit, Ashley. I should be there very soon. I promise. Sit tight baby, I'm coming." I don't get to answer him before another contraction hits and I realize that Dr. Marcus was right. Things are about to get very intense.

Chapter Twenty One

TANNER

I CAN FEEL her pain through the phone and I've had enough of this bullshit traffic.

"I'll be there before you know it, sweet girl. Just keep on breathing like they told you in class." I disconnect with Ash because I don't want her to worry about me while she's in labor and I know she will once she hears my question for Alex.

"Is the shoulder clear? I'm done waiting. Let the cops pull me over. They can issue my tickets or lock me up after I've gotten to the hospital." I ask him, checking my mirror to see if I can really pull this off. I've never been happier to be in the right lane in my life.

His head swivels, looking behind us and in front of us making sure everything is still clear. "There's some lights and shit up there, but I think it's after the exit. I say go for it. It's only about half a mile. Hopefully, the exit is clear."

As soon as Alex says to go for it, I pull onto the shoulder and floor it without hesitation. I have better things to do at the moment. Maybe if I get pulled over, the cop will be a football fan and I'll get a personal escort to the hospital. Not likely, but at this point, I don't give a shit. We hit our exit and everything's a blur as I focus on solely getting to the hospital.

As I finally set my eyes on the front of the hospital, the tightness is my chest starts to ease just slightly. *Almost there, baby.*

The tires screech as I come to an abrupt stop in front of the main doors to the hospital and practically throw my keys at the valet. I don't even check to see if Alex is with me. He's a big boy and can find his own way.

Rushing through the door, I barely stop at the front desk as I ask, "Which way to labor and delivery? My wife is in labor and was just admitted."

"Take the elevator to the fifth floor. Stop at the first set of double doors and hit the intercom button. Tell them your name and then they will buzz you in." The elderly woman responds with a smile on her face, understanding my urgency.

"Thank you," I shout as I race toward the elevator. I hit the button and it feels like a whole hour passes before I hear the ding signaling the elevator has finally arrived. I stab the button for the fifth floor and repeatedly hit the close door button hoping that it will speed this shit up.

"Dude, chill! We're here. Breaking the elevator won't get you there any faster. You'll be with her in less than five minutes," Alex says settling across from me on the other side of the elevator.

"I'll chill when I am standing next to Ashley," I snap.

I follow the receptionist's directions through the double doors and give my name when asked. I'm buzzed through and the nurses at the nurse's station on the other side of the door point me to Ashley's room.

"You're just in time," the older nurse with a gray bun says as she opens the door.

I don't really process what she says until I get through the door and into Ashley's room.

"You're fully dilated, Ashley," Dr. Marcus says from his spot between Ashley's spread legs. "We're going to get everything set up and then you'll start pushing and we'll give this little one a birthday."

The nurse wasn't kidding when she said that I made it just in time. *Holy shit!* I rush over to the bed and grab Ashley's hand since her eyes are closed and she hasn't noticed me yet. Poor thing probably thought I was going to miss the whole thing.

"I'm here, baby. I'm here. I'm so sorry," I tell her bending down to kiss her head. A tear slip from her eye as she grips my hand with what feels like super human strength.

"I was so worried you weren't going to make it," she says now sobbing. "It hurts so bad, but all I could focus on was you not being here."

"Nothing could ever stop me from being here when you bring our little girl into the world. I'm so sorry that I wasn't here for the whole thing, but I'm here now. Tell me what you need." I say stroking her hair. She's sweating and cold at the same time.

"You. I just need you."

"Ashley," Dr. Marcus interrupts. "Things are about to become even more intense. We're all set up and ready to bring this baby into the world. But you have to do the work for me. Okay?"

Ashley doesn't verbally answer but just nods her head.

"Okay, on the next contraction I want you to push. You're going to grab the backs of your thighs and bear down like you're going to the bathroom," the doctor instructs her.

"Alright, on that note I'm going to wait in the waiting room," Alex says from behind me. I totally forgot that he was even here with me. My sole focus was just on getting here to this room, with this woman and this baby.

I will never forget the next sixty minutes for the rest of my life. There was a lot of screaming. Each scream killed me, chipping away at a small part of me. Watching my wife screaming in agony, knowing

I could do nothing to take the pain away was one of the hardest things I've ever endured.

"I'm tired. I can't do this anymore," she had said after about forty-five minutes of pushing.

I brushed the sweat from her forehead with a wet rag. "You're doing great, baby. You can do this. I know you can. Don't give up on me now."

"It hurts so much, Tanner. I don't think I can handle anymore. I swear this baby is ripping me apart." Her sad eyes made me wish I had a vagina so I could do all the work for her. I hated seeing her struggle and not being able to do a thing about it.

Before I could respond another contraction hit and Ash started to push again. "I can see the head, Ashley." Dr. Marcus told her. "Give me another push."

"I can't," she screamed. Her face was beat red and she was struggling to drag oxygen into her lungs.

I couldn't stand to see her hurting anymore. "Ashley, you push our daughter out now. You can do it. I know you can. We've been waiting forever to meet this little one. Don't you dare give up. Let's meet our daughter."

Less than ten minutes later, I heard the most beautiful sound ever. The cry of my little princess. One cry turned my world upside down. I watched as Dr. Marcus held my daughter up and the tears poured from my eyes as if I turned on a faucet.

Holy shit! I'm a father!

Our beautiful princess is a living breathing symbol of my undying love for Ashley. She is love personified.

The picture in front of me, my wife holding our daughter, was well worth all the pain and struggle it took to get here with Ashley. I'd go through it another hundred times over as long as it leads me back here.

"And what are we naming this little beauty?" the nurse with the bun, who's name I've learned is Glenda, asks.

“Michaela Grace Garrison,” Ashley smiles at her while revealing the name we’ve been keeping a secret.

“Michaela?” Quinn questions with a face that shows she’s not all that fond of the name.

“Yes, Michaela,” Ashley confirms.

“Where’d you come up with that one? It wasn’t on any of the lists you told me.” I think Quinn might actually be insulted she wasn’t privy to this name choice.

“It means ‘gift from god’, which is what she is,” Ash explains smiling up at me.

“Yes, she is,” Quinn says now with a smile that lets us know she gets it. “Thanks for letting me be here during that but I need a breather after witnessing that miracle,” she says with a shudder, causing everyone in the room to laugh.

“She’s beautiful,” Ashley says with a look that speaks volumes of the absolute, unconditional love she feels for our daughter.

“Yes, she is,” I say running a hand through Ashley’s tangled hair. “Can I hold my daughter now?”

Ashley begrudgingly lets me take our daughter from her arms, and the minute this little blessing is in my arms, I know I’m a goner. Everything about her is complete perfection.

“Hello, Michaela, its daddy,” I say, bringing my face down to kiss my daughter. “I’ve waited forever to meet you.” I can’t help the emotion that chokes me. This feeling of love is different from every other love I’ve ever felt. It’s all consuming and makes you want to make the world a better place so that this child in your arms never feels an ounce of sadness or pain. I’d walk through fire for these ladies. I’d live in hell as long as they were safe. Nothing will ever touch my family. My heart swells in my chest.

“You’re beautiful and perfect, Princess,” I tell her. “Just like your mommy.” I glance at Ashley to see her wiping away her tears, which, like mine, are flowing freely down her face.

"You're amazing," I say to Ashley. "Thank you so much for being my best friend, my biggest supporter, my lover and my wife. Thank you so much for giving me her. Thank you for completing me."

Epilogue

QUINN

AS ALEX WALKS into the room, I wish I would've reminded myself during the chaos of Ashley going into labor to prepare for having to see him again. It's been two years since I've seen him, but it also feels like the wedding was just yesterday. Leave it to Ash to go into labor in dramatic fashion and catch us all off guard. I guess I never expected to see him here, but then again why wouldn't I? We have always been a staple in Ash and Tanner's life, well until I did what needed to be done. I don't regret what I did to Alex, but I can't say that I don't miss him. He really is an amazing guy, but we'll never be on the same page. I thought we were once, but I couldn't have been more wrong!

His beautiful hazel eyes lock on mine. We're currently in a staring match as I stand next to Ashley's bed rocking a beautiful little Michaela. Ash nodded off about two minutes after I snatched the fluffy little bundle of pink from her arms and Tanner needed to go make a few calls to his family. Without buffers, there's nothing to cut the tension between Alex and me.

I break first, casting my gaze to the little princess curled up in my chest. I can't stop the reel of images of us that quickly passes through my mind. What we had was combustible, undeniable passion. God, the way we used to come together was fucking amazing! Nothing will ever compare to it, but what's done is done and it's time to move on.

Shaking my thoughts free, I force myself to remember why I had to end things to begin with. I meet his eyes once more, intending to offer up a small smile to taper down the tension in the room, but instead, I find hard eyes. Anger swirling in the waves of brown and green. His eyes dart to my left hand, which is currently rubbing little circles on Michaela's back, then back to my eyes. His knuckles turn white as they grip the bed rail before he pushes off and leaves the room in a huff.

I look down and catch a glimpse of the huge five and a half karat diamond engagement ring on my left ring finger. Guess the cat's out of the bag now. I had forgotten about my engagement in the whirl of activity today. It's for the best. I'm sorry he's upset, but I still don't regret a thing. Being with Alex was a dangerous thing for me.

It's A Girl!

WELCOMED WITH LOVE
Michaela Grace Garrison
A
B
C
JULY 22ND 7LBS. 2OZ 21INCHES

Acknowledgements

First and foremost, I have to thank my incredible readers for even making this story possible. If it wasn't for you guys and your love for Ashley and Tanner, this series wouldn't have gotten this far. So please give yourselves a pat on the back for being the best readers ever.

As with all my books, Freed wouldn't have been half the book it was without the unbelievable support of Isabelle Richards. You, my dear, are the rock of my writing career. You push and push until my writing is the best it can be. I can always count on you to tell me what I need to hear, even when I don't want to. You are the best friend and writing partner any one could ever ask for. I don't know what I ever did to deserve your support but I'd do it over and over again! I love you!

Yolanda, you didn't know me from a hole in the wall but you have supported me in anything and everything since the very beginning! I'm so glad that you fell in love with Tanner. You are amazing and thank you for everything that you do.

Tiffany, my little pussy. You are the queen of all things pretty. Thank you for making all the wonderful teasers and graphics for me, even when you wanted to kill me! I'm so glad that you're a shy little chicken shit and that I have no qualms about yelling 'pussy' in a crowded room of people! Love you bitch!

Dessuré, you dirty slut, I freaking love you! Thank you for your support and your awesome promo skills. Thank you for being a genuinely nice person and doing all the little things you have done for me. They may seem small to you but to me they mean the world.

Kari, thank you so much for a wonderful cover. Thank you for dealing with my indecisiveness and constant switching of things. I'm sure I drove you mad! But the cover is amazing!! Mwah!

Leslie, thank you for working your ass off on the edits for this one!! It was such a pleasure working with you again. I'm glad it was under less rushed circumstances this time!

Joe, thank you for all your input in making sure all my football stuff was not only awesome but one hundred percent realistic. I can get crazy when it comes to football so thanks for helping me reign it in. And thank you for thanking me for asking for your help!! That made me feel really special!

Last but not least, thank you to my husband for putting up with my craziness while writing. Thanks for putting up with the crappy dinners, lack of clean laundry and messy house while I was trying to put these books together. But let's face it, I've never been a good cook or a good housekeeper. Love you!

About The Author

Kimberly is a stay at home mom to four beautiful, crazy children by day and a steaming hot novelist by night. She's a Jersey girl at heart and that's where she currently calls home with her amazing husband and children.

Her debut release Inhibitions and the subsequent Uninhibited Series as well as the spin-off Apprehensive Duet both show her love of all things football. But not to worry, she'll still bring you plenty of steam!

When not writing she can be found curled up with a good book or watching her beloved New York Jets. Lover all things romance, including a little M/M action as well as the dark and twisted. She enjoys video chats with her best friends and always loves to hear from her fans on social media.

Connect with Kimberly
Website: www.BERGBOOKS.com
Facebook: www.facebook.com/authorkaberg
Facebook Fan Group: Kimberly's Knockout Fangirls
Twitter: @AuthorKaberg
Instagram: @AuthorKaberg

88217482R00072

Made in the USA
Columbia, SC
02 February 2018